Sam felt as if   world on his shoulders,

trying to keep the farm going and take care of his son.

He did not need a woman moving in next door and complicating things.

Especially a woman who had a way of igniting feelings and emotions he had sworn never to feel for any woman, ever again.

He would just have to stop thinking about how it made him feel all warm inside when Jackie Lundigan smiled at him, or how her bright, friendly eyes were as green as new spring grass. And to stop thinking how good it would feel to touch her, hold her and—

Sam gave his head a vicious shake.

It would be hard, but she would not be around much longer.

At least, that was how he hoped it would be, because he did not want to think of the consequences if she stayed....

Dear Reader,

Welcome to Special Edition…where each month we offer six wonderfully emotional romances about people just like you—striving to find the perfect balance between life, career, family and, of course, love.…

To start off, Susan Mallery shines with her thirtieth Silhouette novel, *Surprise Delivery*. In this not-to-be-missed THAT'S MY BABY! title, a very pregnant heroine is stuck in an elevator with a charming stranger—and is about to give birth!

Love proves to be the greatest adventure of all in *Hunter's Pride* by Lindsay McKenna. In the continuation of her enthralling MORGAN'S MERCENARIES: THE HUNTERS series, fiercely proud Devlin Hunter is teamed up with a feisty beauty who challenges him at every turn. And don't miss the wonderful romance between a harried single dad and a spirited virgin in *The Home Love Built* by Christine Flynn.

Next, a compassionate paralegal reunites a brooding cop with his twin sons in *The Fatherhood Factor*—book three in Diana Whitney's heartwarming FOR THE CHILDREN series. Then a lovely newcomer befriends her neighbor's little boy and breaks through to the lad's guarded dad in *My Child, Our Child* by *New York Times* bestselling author Patricia Hagan.

Finally this month, Tracy Sinclair pens *The Bachelor King*, a regally romantic tale about a powerful king who marries a "pregnant" American beauty, only to receive the royal shock of his life!

I hope you enjoy these six unforgettable romances created *by* women like you, *for* women like you!

Sincerely,

Karen Taylor Richman
Senior Editor

Please address questions and book requests to:
Silhouette Reader Service
U.S.: 3010 Walden Ave., P.O. Box 1325, Buffalo, NY 14269
Canadian: P.O. Box 609, Fort Erie, Ont. L2A 5X3

PATRICIA HAGAN

MY CHILD, OUR CHILD

Silhouette®

SPECIAL EDITION®

Published by Silhouette Books
America's Publisher of Contemporary Romance

To James W. Ralph, M.D. Col, MC, MFS-Ret.,
with thanks and appreciation for his assistance in
providing the medical facts for this story.
However, I take responsibility for poetic license.

 SILHOUETTE BOOKS

ISBN 0-373-24277-8

MY CHILD, OUR CHILD

Copyright © 1999 by Patricia Hagan

Printed in U.S.A.

Books by Patricia Hagan

Silhouette Special Edition

Bride for Hire #1127
My Child, Our Child #1277

Yours Truly

Boy Re-Meets Girl
Groom on the Run

Harlequin Historicals

The Daring #84
The Desire #143

PATRICIA HAGAN

New York Times bestselling author Patricia Hagan had written and published over 2,500 short stories before selling her first book in 1971. With a background in English and journalism from the University of Alabama, Pat has won awards for radio, television, newspaper and magazine writing. Her hobbies include reading, painting and cooking. The author and her Norwegian husband, Erik, divide their time between their Florida retreat in Boca Raton and their home in Bergen, Norway.

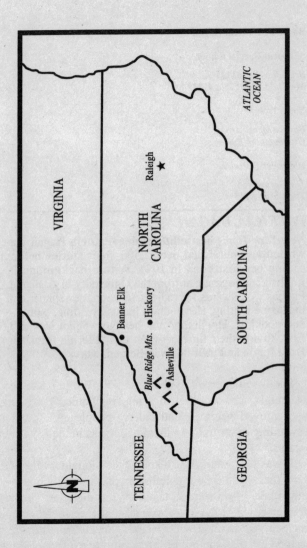

Chapter One

The aroma of fresh-brewed coffee greeted Jackie Lundigan as she entered the back door of Dove Haven Rest Home. The luscious smell of blueberry pancakes told her it was Wednesday, because, as dietician, she could tell the day of the week by whatever odor wafted from the kitchen.

She loved everything about her job. While some people might find working in a nursing home depressing, she enjoyed being around elderly people and found it rewarding to try to bring them happiness in their twilight years.

It was also gratifying to know, she thought with pride, how there would be few leftovers on this day's menu or any other. When she had taken over as dietician, she had implemented a program whereby the residents could have a say in their diet. Regular meetings with them helped her plan the bill of fare, ensuring everyone would have their favorite foods. Accordingly, she had managed to balance out everything nutritionally, and the culinary offerings at Dove Haven were highly praised, not only by residents but their family members, as well.

Her office was opposite the kitchen, but she went first to the staff break room. It was a bright, cheery place, with comfortable sofas and chairs, long tables for meals or snacks, a refrigerator to store personal food, and vending machines for soft drinks and the junk food even she sometimes craved.

Long, wide windows offered a view to the park area in the rear where, weather permitting, those residents who were able to be up and about could enjoy the fresh air.

On the wall next to the door there were several rows of pigeonhole boxes where staff received mail and memos. Hers was full, as usual, because every food vendor in the county was constantly trying to woo Dove Haven's business through her.

Sipping her coffee, she leafed through the envelopes and flyers, trashing most. She had her favorite vendors, so there was no need to change…no need to waste her time reading about others.

Then she saw the blue phone memo with the notation that Dottie Benjamin had called. She found that odd, because, after Jackie's breakup, Dottie and Chuck had abandoned her like most of the couples she and Kevin had hung out with during their marriage. But that had not come as a surprise since the guys were all Kevin's buddies.

Folding the memo, she slipped it into the pocket of her white smock. Maybe Dottie had decided to keep in touch, after all. But according to what the receptionist had entered in the time box, the call came early—right at 7:00 a.m.—and Jackie found that even more bizarre.

She also wondered about it being marked "urgent," but not enough to make her return the call anytime soon. After all, she had a full day's work ahead and did not want to start it off by being reminded of Kevin in any way. Besides, everything had been taken care of. She had signed the separation agreement prepared by his lawyer. Under North Carolina law, a divorce would be granted when they had been apart for at least a year. The healing process had begun, and she did not want to re-open the wounds.

She had tried to push it out of her mind—how she had worked all those years to put him through medical school. Sure, he'd had it tough with hard studies and long hours as an intern, but life had been no bed of roses for her, either.

They had married after graduating from high school. Kevin's father had mortgaged his house to pay his tuition but that was the only help they'd had. Her parents were dead, and she had gone to work as a kitchen helper at Dove Haven to pay for the rent and groceries. Eventually, because she worked her buns off, she had managed to get certification as a dietician by going to night school.

She could not pinpoint exactly when the trouble started…when they began to drift apart. Things weren't too bad during college and medical school, but once he began his residency, he made her feel out of place in his world. At parties he would tell her to watch what she said, lest she embarrass him. People, especially doctors, he chided, didn't want to hear her warm and fuzzy stories about old people. He was also critical of her hair, her clothes, seeming to constantly look for—and find—fault.

At first, she had tried, really tried, to please him and live up to the way he felt a future surgeon's wife should behave. But pretense had never been her style. She took a good, hard look at herself, liked what she saw and refused to be something she wasn't. She was not, by God, ashamed to like old people or to volunteer to help out at the local animal shelter when time permitted—all of which led to more belittlement from Kevin.

Still, she felt like she had done everything she could to try and hold the marriage together, but nothing seemed to work. Eventually he had begun to sleep on the sofa in the living room of their tiny one-bedroom apartment. At first he said it was because he came in at all hours from his crazy shifts, but then he started staying out all night when she knew he wasn't working or studying, and she feared the end might be near.

And it came when he finished his residency.

Without fanfare or discussion, he declared that he wanted a divorce and promptly moved out.

At first, she had been stunned…devastated…and, yes, broken-hearted. For in the back of her mind, she had dared to think that once the grueling demands of internship and residency were behind him, they could, by some miracle, find a way to recapture the love that had led them to marriage in the first place.

But in the three weeks since he had moved out, she was surprised to realize that nothing about her existence had really changed. He had never been around, anyway, and their sex life had dwindled to the point she could not even remember the last time they had made love.

Perhaps more surprising than Kevin wanting a divorce was how he agreed to take over all their debts—huge credit card bills he had amassed, which she was also responsible for paying.

When she asked, wide-eyed with wonder, how he was able to be so benevolent, he had blithely explained he had accepted an offer to join the practice of a prominent surgeon in Winston-Salem. A generous advance on his earnings was part of the deal, so he wanted a clean break. He was starting a new life, he happily boasted, and did not intend to take any baggage from his old one along.

Well, she wanted a new life, too, she thought with bitterness rising. For too long everything had revolved around Kevin—*his* wants and needs. Now she would finally have time for hers. She wanted to paint, dabble in pottery, maybe write poetry—all the things Kevin had scorned as a waste of her time. But though she now had the time, and would like nothing better than to start over somewhere else, it was financially impossible. She had no savings, and she still had her car to pay for—even though it was about as feeble as some of the nursing home residents. But maybe one day...

"So this is why you aren't answering your phone." Maxine Dwyer, the receptionist, breezed into the room and headed for the coffeepot. "I've buzzed you a couple of times. That Benjamin woman called again. She sounds real excited. Says she's got to talk to you."

"I'll go call her now. Thanks."

"No problem." Maxine snatched up a bagel on her way out.

Jackie began gathering up the rest of the mail she'd not yet been through, but before she could finish, Betsy Reidy stuck her head in the door, waving a sheet of paper. "Here's the tray list. Want me to leave it on your desk? I've got to run."

Jackie frowned. "Run where?" She had hired Betsy as an aide in the kitchen only a week ago, but she did not seem to be working out. She was always late and twice had claimed emergencies to leave the job for a few hours.

"Car trouble. I've got to go to the factory where my husband works and get some money from him to pay the bill before the garage will fix it. He got an advance on his salary, and—"

Jackie held out her hand to take the paper. "Just do it, Betsy. And please try to get back as soon as you can. Lunch is only a few hours away, remember? And they need you in the kitchen." She did not want to seem unsympathetic but felt most of Betsy's problems were exaggerated. She also suspected she seized every opportunity to get out of having to work during the busiest times.

"Oh, I will, I will." Betsy walked over to the table as though she had all the time in the world and began wrapping bagels in paper napkins. "I guess it's okay for me to take a couple of these to Buddy. They always go stale, anyway, 'cause nobody around here wants them."

Jackie was not listening, busy scanning the check-off sheet for breakfast. The amount a patient ate and drank at each meal was noted and kept in a log. It was important, not only to know how much nutrition they were getting but to judge any change in appetite that could signal problems.

Betsy was almost out the door when one special name leaped out at Jackie. "Wait a minute. How come Miss Pratt didn't touch her tray?"

"Miss Pratt?" Betsy seemed not to recognize the name. "I don't know. What's marked?"

"Zero consumed. That's strange. Miss Pratt always has a huge appetite."

Betsy shrugged. "You'll have to ask somebody else. I don't know anything about it."

"Well, I'll go check on her right now." Jackie hurriedly gathered her things.

Libby Pratt was not only one of her favorite people, she was a special friend. They had grown quite close in the years since Libby had come to Dove Haven. In fact, she had lent a compassionate ear when Jackie felt the need to talk to someone about her failing marriage.

She had also felt deeply sorry for the cruel blow life had dealt Libby. Never having married, she had dedicated herself to her career as a history teacher. It had been her dream upon retirement to travel the world, visiting the places she had spent so many years teaching others about. With no family, she was all alone in the world, but she was a spunky soul and had no trepidation over traveling by herself. But before her adventures could begin, a traffic accident had left her crippled, forcing her into a nursing home and ending her dreams.

Taking a bagel to munch on later, Jackie left the break room. Seeing one of the other kitchen workers coming out of the rest room, she asked, "Harriet, what's the story with Miss Pratt?" Protocol required that residents not be referred to by a first name, regardless of the relationship with an employee. "She's marked zero percent eaten. Is she still in the dining room?"

"She didn't show at all. The tray just sat there."

Alarm and concern triggered a sharp retort. "Well, didn't anyone find out why? When a patient doesn't show, somebody is supposed to find out the reason. Who's the CNA on that wing this week?"

Harriet fired back, "How should I know? I work in the kitchen, remember?"

She walked away, rounded a corner and disappeared.

Hurrying on into her office, Jackie dropped the mail on her desk. A few pieces fell to the floor, but she stepped over them in her haste to go and check on Libby. Everything else could wait till she found out what was going on.

The phone rang.

She kept on going.

The building was shaped like a cross, four wings branching out to separate residents by need. Libby was in the domiciliary wing, which meant that while she had special needs, she was not infirm enough to be considered a nursing patient. With a walker, she was able to get around slowly on her own. She did not like the confines of her room and it was not an unusual sight to see her out and about. She attended almost every activity scheduled and made it a point to visit the bedridden to offer company and cheer.

Given all that, Jackie feared there had to be something seriously wrong for Libby not to have shown up for breakfast.

No one was around the nurses' station, situated in the middle of the cross. But as she turned towards Libby's wing, one of the CNAs saw her and called, "Maxine is looking for you. She just called here to ask if we'd seen you. She says some woman is having kittens trying to catch up with you."

Jackie did not slow her pace as she spoke over her shoulder, "I don't have time right now. If she calls again, please tell her—"

The phone on the counter rang.

"That's gonna be her again," the CNA said with a

frown. "Nurse Vincent is busy with a patient who's really bad off, and I'm supposed to be answering the phone, and I'm going to get way behind on my work if I have to keep taking calls from the receptionist looking for you."

Jackie groaned and turned back. Too many people were being inconvenienced, so there was nothing to do but take the call.

Lifting the receiver, she told Maxine to put it through, and a second later she heard Dottie's excited voice, "Oh, thank God, Jackie. I was afraid I wouldn't be able to reach you before you hear it from somebody else."

Jackie tensed. "Hear what?"

"It's Kevin."

She felt a twinge of apprehension. "What's wrong? Is he hurt?"

Dottie's laugh was sharp, brittle. "No, nothing like that, but when you hear what he's done you might wish he were."

Jackie doubted that. She was not the sort to wish misfortune on anyone, regardless. "Well, suppose you tell me what this is all about, Dottie, because I'm real busy around here."

She heard Dottie take a deep breath, then, "Okay, here goes—he's getting married this weekend."

Jackie gripped the phone before it could slip though her fingers. "What are you talking about? We aren't divorced and won't be for a year."

"He went to Mexico and got a quickie."

Jackie leaned against the desk, one hand pressing against her suddenly throbbing temple. "I don't understand. I mean, I've always thought Mexican divorces weren't legal in North Carolina."

"Only if somebody protests, and you can bet your last

pair of run-free panty hose he's praying you won't, because from what he told Chuck, his bride is almost four months pregnant.''

''What bride?'' She forced her wobbling legs to move her around the counter so she could collapse in a chair before they gave way. ''I mean—who is she? None of this makes any sense.''

Dottie snorted. ''I guess not. It was a big blow to Chuck, too. Kevin called him this morning to tell him the news. He wants all his buddies to drive to Winston-Salem this weekend for the wedding his bride's family is putting on. I understand it's going to be quite lavish, despite the circumstances. Chuck has to rent a tux, and I've got to buy a new dress. The bride's parents are having it at their country club.''

She swayed. Dear God, what was going on here? ''Does the...the bride have a name?'' she managed to ask with a shaky laugh.

''Yeah. Mimi Faulkner.''

The Faulkner part was familiar, and Jackie squeezed her eyes shut, waiting for the bell of recognition to ring. When it did, her eyes flew open and she spoke so loudly two CNAs down the hall turned to stare.

''Dr. Faulkner's daughter. The two-timing creep. Now it all adds up.''

''That's right. Her father is the one Kevin is going into practice with.'' She paused a moment before reluctantly adding, ''Actually, a lot of us wives knew about her, Jackie, but we couldn't say anything to you. You understand, don't you? I mean, we really wanted to, because Kevin was being such a jerk. But when I heard about this, I told Chuck enough was enough. You had to be told, because Kevin will have to let you know, won't he? And this way you can be ready to act like you don't give a damn."

With a sigh of resignation, Jackie quietly said, "Actually, Dottie, I don't give a damn. Now, thanks for calling, but I've really got to get back to work."

She hung up the phone and sat there a few moments, needing time to get herself together. It was true that she no longer cared what he did, but it was still humiliating that she had been the last to know he had been seeing someone else.

And now she understood how he had been able to step into a lucrative practice right out of his surgical residency, not to mention pay off the credit cards. But his girlfriend's pregnancy had complicated things, making the one-year wait for divorce a great inconvenience. So he had flown down to Mexico—future poppa-in-law no doubt footing the bill for that—and was counting on her pride to keep her from making a fuss about it.

And he was right.

"To hell with him," she muttered under her breath and bolted to her feet.

The thing to do was get over it.

Don't go there.

Don't think about how she'd been used, had, humiliated and betrayed.

Look forward. Not back.

With head held high, shoulders squared, eyes straight ahead, she continued down the hall.

Maybe it was time to get serious about the idea she had been toying with ever since Libby mentioned she was thinking about leaving Dove Haven to move into an apartment and have home health care. If they went in together on a large enough place and lived together, Libby wouldn't need anyone to come in at night.

Besides, she had come to love Libby as though she were her own grandmother, and Libby had confided she looked upon her as the granddaughter she'd never had. They would be like family.

Libby could also empathize with her in her despair, for she had suffered anguish in matters of the heart herself, but under different circumstances. Born and raised in the western North Carolina mountains around Banner Elk, Libby had confided how she could not remember a time when she had not loved Roy Colton. And when he had been killed in World War II, she had never been able to love anyone else.

When Libby had talked of the cool, green mountains, sometimes her eyes would become misty. When Jackie had asked why she never went there, when she seemed to love the peace and serenity of her home so deeply, Libby's smile had been both sweet and sad. True, she had explained, she did love the Blue Ridge, but going back had been too painful: there were too many memories…too many ghosts. Still, she had returned periodically as long as her parents were alive, but after they died, she never went back.

Jackie quickened her pace. She hoped Libby was not sick…for many reasons, most of them, she supposed, selfish. She wanted—needed—to tell her the mind-blowing news about Kevin. She also felt the pressing need to persuade her to move somewhere with her, because all of a sudden she understood why Libby had never wanted to go back to the mountains. Only Libby's memories had been sweet. The ones Jackie longed to forget were the ones that made her feel like a complete and utter fool. The sooner she moved out of the home she had shared with Kevin, the quicker the fresh wounds would begin to heal.

Passing the physical therapy room, someone called out to her, and she turned to see it was Vickie Thornton, one of the therapists.

"You've got a phone call."

Jackie came to a halt, fists clenching at her sides. "I swear if management doesn't buy me a pager, I'm going to pay for it myself."

"Maxine said it's important. That's why she's trying to track you down." Vickie was holding the phone in her hand as she leaned out the door.

Jackie groaned. That meant it could only be Dottie, having remembered some other juicy tidbit she wanted to pass along. "Well, I'm busy right now, Vickie. I've got to check on a resident I'm real concerned about. Please just tell Maxine to tell Dottie I promise to call her back later."

"It's not Dottie…whoever Dottie is."

Something in Vickie's voice made the hair stand up on the back of Jackie's neck. "Then tell whoever it is—"

"It's Kevin."

Her legs felt as if they were made of wood as Jackie walked slowly to where Vickie waited. The last thing she wanted right then was to talk to Kevin, but it would best to get it over with.

She took the phone, and Vickie politely left to give her privacy.

She mustered a civil, calm tone. "Yes, Kevin, what is it?"

She heard him take a deep breath. No doubt to gather his courage, the two-timing bastard.

"I've got something to tell you, and I wanted you to hear it from me before word spread."

She let him go on, not about to make it any easier for him by telling him she already knew.

"I got the divorce, Jackie. In Mexico. All I had to do was fly in and spend the night and a judge signed the decree. It's done all the time." He gave a nervous little laugh. "These damn North Carolina laws are so old-fashioned. I mean—what's the point in waiting a whole year when it's over, right? It just causes stress for everybody concerned. We need to get on with our lives, and I figured you'd welcome having it over with as much as me."

"Not quite," she said quietly, coldly. "*I* wasn't in a hurry to get married."

Silence. Then a gasp. "Who…who told you?"

"It doesn't matter."

He went into a defensive mode. "You aren't going to make a big stink over this, are you, Jackie? I mean, hey, it will only make you look bad. Everybody will say you're just being vindictive, and—"

She interrupted him, because he was firing words like bullets. And he was also wasting her time.

"I'd never dream of contesting it, Kevin. I wish you, your bride and the baby you're going to have in about five months, only the best."

"You…you know about that, too," he said lamely.

"Yes. I know about that."

"So how long—"

"Kevin, stop it," she snapped. "This is a waste of time for both of us. It doesn't matter. Nothing about you matters to me, anymore. Now I've told you—I don't intend to protest your quickie divorce, so we have nothing else to discuss. Goodbye."

She hung up the phone and realized she felt better

than she had in ages. She was actually glad he had called, so she could have the satisfaction of letting him know that, despite everything, she didn't have enough feelings left for him to care what he did.

Because now closure could begin.

"Thanks, Vickie," she said as the therapist came out of a supply closet, as if on cue.

"No problem. Listen, I'm sorry to hear about—"

"You *know?*" Jackie had started for the door but whirled about. "Oh, my God, how many others?" She shook her head and blinked back tears of humiliation. "It really is true, isn't it? That the wife is always the last to know?"

She hurried on out.

Vickie rushed to the door. "What are you talking about? I don't think we're talking about the same thing...."

Jackie stepped around kitchen helpers retrieving breakfast trays and maneuvered around CNAs rolling residents to showers or outdoors to enjoy the sunny day.

Libby's room was at the very end of the hall. Jackie knew she was probably being selfish to hope against hope her dear friend felt like talking, because never had she needed a sympathetic ear more.

She slowed, apprehension creeping.

Libby's door was closed.

And that was highly unusual, because, unless she was dressing or undressing, she left it open as an invitation for anyone to come inside. She was just that kind of person—warm, genial, ready to be a friend.

She started to knock, but her hand froze in midair as she heard a sad voice softly call, "There's no need, Miss Jackie."

Turning slowly, fearfully, she met the tearful gaze of

Winnie Porter, the lady who lived in the room opposite Libby's.

"She died sometime last night. I was awake when they came by and closed all our doors so we wouldn't see them take her away."

Jackie stared at her for a few seconds, numb and disbelieving, then somehow remembered to disengage the door alarm as she stumbled outside.

Lowering to Libby's bench, she covered her hands with her face and wept.

Something nudged her leg. Something warm and fuzzy.

She glanced down to see the little fat squirrel Libby had tamed.

Perhaps it was her imagination…her grief making her mind play tricks, but something in his eyes seemed to mirror sadness over having also lost a dear friend.

Through her tears she reached into her pocket and took out the bagel she had put there earlier.

The squirrel eagerly took it from her hand and scampered away.

His life would go on without Libby.

And so would hers.

But, dear Lord, it was going to be so very hard…for never, ever, had she felt so alone.

Chapter Two

Jackie thought the memorial service held in Dove Haven's chapel was sweet and charming…just as Libby had been.

Late-summer flowers, marigolds and pansies, decorated the altar where residents who had loved her took turns sharing how much brighter their lives were for having known her.

Jackie could have contributed much from her own experience with Libby but felt it more important for the others to have their say.

During the service she noticed a man sitting nearby and wondered if he were a distant relative, then remembered Libby had no family. He was probably a friend Jackie never had a chance to meet.

At last it was over. Madeline Stallings, Dove Haven's director, invited everyone to a reception in the recreation room. Jackie hurried to be the first out of the door, want-

ing to make sure the special refreshments she had asked
the kitchen staff to make were ready.

Jackie went to the white linen-covered table and began ladling a lime sherbet and ginger ale punch, Libby's
favorite, into paper cups. When there was no one else to
be served, she took a cup for herself. Then she noticed
the same man, standing to one side.

He walked over to her and pleasantly said, "You're
Jackie Lundigan, aren't you? Miss Pratt pointed you out
to me once when I was visiting her, but there wasn't
opportunity for introductions."

Jackie politely responded, "And I remember seeing
you, but she never told me who you were."

He handed her a card, and she read the name: "James
Burkhalter, Attorney at law."

"I would appreciate it if you'd call my office for an
appointment. We need to talk," he said.

She looked at the card again, then at him. "And what
is this all about?"

"I was Miss Pratt's attorney. I made her will for her."

Nonplussed, she asked, "Well, what does that have to
do with me?"

"You're in it," he said quietly and walked away.

Aimlessly Jackie leafed through the outdated magazine, glancing often at her watch.

The receptionist noticed and apologized, "I'm so
sorry, Miss Lundigan. I have no idea what's keeping Mr.
Burkhalter. He said he'd only be at the courthouse a few
minutes."

"It's all right. I'm in no hurry." And she wasn't. Mrs.
Stallings had told her she could have the rest of the day
off, but curiosity was needling her. What could Libby's
will have to do with her? An animal lover, Libby had

told her she was leaving everything to the local shelter's building fund. Jackie hoped she hadn't changed her mind. She had not befriended Libby for monetary compensation. Still, if Libby had seen fit to leave her something of sentimental value to remember her by, she would be grateful and honored.

The outer door to the office opened and James Burkhalter breezed in.

"I am so sorry to keep you waiting." He held out a welcoming hand as Jackie rose from her chair. "I ran into a judge I'd been trying to talk to for days and had to take advantage of it. Come on in, please."

He hurried to his desk and laid down the manila folders and yellow legal pad he had been carrying. "Just have a seat and make yourself comfortable." He started leafing through stacks of papers on his desk.

She sat down and drank in the smell of leather from the sofa as well as the bound volumes of law digests lining floor-to-ceiling shelves on two walls.

She found herself growing impatient and uncomfortable with the situation. She had heard too many stories about how some unscrupulous care givers manipulated old people into naming them in their wills. She did not want to be thought one of them. Never, not once, had she befriended Libby—or any other resident at Dove Haven—for any reason other than how good it made her feel. She neither expected, nor wanted, anything in return.

"Ah, here it is—Libby Pratt's last will and testament. I'm just waiting for the copy of her death certificate to file it for probate. She died a peaceful death, didn't she? In her sleep. The way most of us would prefer to go. A heart attack, I was told."

Suddenly Jackie could stand it no longer and said,

"Mr. Burkhalter, there must be some mistake. Libby—Miss Pratt—told me she was leaving everything to the local animal shelter. And I think that's wonderful. I never wanted anything from her, and—"

"I know that." Leaning back in his chair, he templed his fingers as he looked at her over the glasses perched on the end of his nose. "She told me all about you...how kind you were to her...how much your friendship meant." He smiled, eyes twinkling. "She also told me you would argue about this."

"Not if it's something sentimental. Beyond that, I'd have to refuse. In my position I can't afford to have a resident leave me money."

"It's not money."

She relaxed a little. That meant some kind of memento and that was fine. "Well, that's a relief. Is it the little rolling pin? I'll treasure that, believe me."

"Yes, she left you that...and something else."

Jackie was truly puzzled then.

Suddenly he asked, "Did Libby ever tell you about Roy Colton?"

"Yes. I know he was the one great love of her life, and when he was killed in the war, she never got over it."

"No, she didn't. She devoted herself to her work and became one of the finest teachers I ever knew."

Jackie knew then his visits to see Libby had not been altogether business. "Then you were one of her students?"

"Yes, and both of my children, as well. And she was wonderful. She made history come alive. I wish you could have known her then, Mrs. Lundigan. She was truly extraordinary, and a lot of people grieved when her dreams for retirement ended so tragically.

''I was pleased when she contacted me to draw up her new will,'' he continued, picking up the blue-backed document once more. ''Then she told me the story about Roy Colton. I'd wondered why she never married, but when I heard about their romance and his tragic death, I understood. And when she told me how much she thought of you, I also understand why she wanted to change her will.''

''But you said she wasn't leaving me money.''

He held up a hand. ''Please, hear me out. We aren't talking about money. We're talking about something that Roy Colton left her in his will that she never wanted to be sold.''

Curiosity was killing her. ''And what might that be?''

''A Christmas tree farm.''

''A Christmas tree farm?'' she echoed with a laugh. ''She never told me she had one. And what am I supposed to do with it?'' Then the thought struck, and she cried, ''Of course. I'll just sell it and turn the money over to the animal shelter.''

He shook his head. ''She was explicit that it was not to be sold. If you don't want it, then it will go on as it has been—run by a neighbor, the profits turned over to the shelter.''

She shrugged. ''Then that's what I'll do—turn it down and the shelter will get the money.''

He stared at her long and hard, then said, with reluctance, ''She told me about your marital problems.''

Jackie stiffened. ''I wish she hadn't, but it doesn't matter. I don't have them anymore. I'm divorced.''

He shifted uncomfortably in his chair. ''I wasn't supposed to let you know that I knew, but she said if you did refuse, I was to tell you that it was a chance for a new beginning for you—a new life. She wanted you to have an adventure.

"You see," he went on to explain, "there's a little cabin on the land, along with a few outbuildings. You could make your home there if you like. Granted, according to Libby, it's very remote." He grinned. "A hundred acres more or less certainly would be, so don't plan on having pizza delivered."

Jackie stared at him, overwhelmed. A hundred acres. A cabin. The serene beauty of the mountains. It was something she had only dreamed about—a place where she could do the things she loved as well as commune with nature. The idea suddenly seemed terribly intriguing.

She bit her lip thoughtfully. "I don't know what to say. I mean, it sounds wonderful, and I guess I'd be a fool to turn it down."

Blandly he pointed out, "Not really. No one could expect you to give up your job to go live in the middle of nowhere. I told Libby that, but she disagreed. She seemed to think a 180-degree turnaround in your life was exactly what you might want."

How right she was, Jackie thought, and that was even before she knew about Kevin and his pregnant bride.

He opened a desk drawer and took out the carved rolling pin. Jackie had helped pack what few personal belongings Libby had in her room at Dove Haven, and the wooden object had been among them.

"I took the liberty of sending everything else to Good Will," he said, handing over the rolling pin. "You can go ahead and take this. It doesn't have any monetary value, so I don't need it for probate. But as soon as you make up your mind about the tree farm, I'd appreciate your telling me so I can start the ball rolling in another direction should you turn it down.''

''I'm not going to.'' Her tone was so forceful it surprised even her, and she saw that Mr. Burkhalter also seemed a bit taken aback.

With a deep breath of resolve she continued, ''I'm going to give notice, have a giant yard sale, pack my clothes and head for the mountains. Libby was right. I am ready for a 180-degree change.''

She started to get up, but he signaled her to stay where she was.

She settled back with a tiny wave of foreboding.

''There's something else.''

Her brow furrowed warily.

''Actually, you will only own half the farm.''

Some of her enthusiasm dimmed. ''I don't understand.''

''As she explained it to me, Roy Colton's only sibling was a brother. The two of them were to inherit the land together when their father died. From what she told me, she hadn't been back in nearly fifty years. Someone else ran the farm. Maybe a descendent of Roy Colton's brother. She didn't say. Maybe she didn't know. Anyway, she received her share of the profits once a year and didn't care how the place was run. I imagine you'd want to continue the same arrangement since you wouldn't know what you were doing.

''Just sit back, collect the money, and let someone else do all the work,'' he finished with a grin.

Jackie knew, even though it was all happening so fast, that she had no intention of not taking an active part in running the farm. The thought of growing Christmas trees sounded like fun. Besides, owning half a farm was better than nothing. ''Do I have to decide now if I want to do that—keep the same arrangement she had, I mean?''

''No. You can take care of all that when you get there. But take some time to think it over and make sure it's what you want.''

''I already have. How soon can I claim my share?''

He looked surprised that she had made up her mind so quickly and, after a moment's hesitation, said, ''Well, I suppose I can have the probate judge issue a contingency deed. The estate won't be completely settled for six months, but I see no problem if you want to move in before then. Just when would you like to?''

Her enthusiasm shone in her smile. ''Right after the yard sale.''

Chapter Three

Crude wooden fruit stands with tin roofs dotted the sides of the roads, flanked by baskets of red and gold apples along with stacks of bright orange pumpkins.

It was the best time of year to be moving to the mountains, and Jackie was so excited that sometimes thinking about the future make her hands shake as she clutched the steering wheel.

Or was it the car that was actually shaking? She frowned. With the odometer over the hundred-thousand mark, the old clunker had been breathing its last for quite a while. She had been planning to trade it since Kevin had paid off the credit cards, freeing up her paycheck for other expenses. Now, however, with no job, she had to be careful with what money she had. She would not receive any of Libby's share of the profits from this year's tree harvest until the estate was probated and that was months away. So a new car before then was out of the question.

She had not told anyone at Dove Haven where she was going. Neither had she told them about Libby leaving her the farm. Too much was already known about her private life, it seemed, so she merely turned in her notice, said she was taking a year's sabbatical and left.

So, with each mile the past faded farther and farther in the rearview mirror of her mind, and she concentrated on looking ahead, envisioning the kind of peaceful, tranquil life she had always dreamed about.

At last she was in the heart of the Blue Ridge mountains, heading northeast toward the Tennessee state line.

The road curved north, sometimes seeming to tunnel through a veritable army of sentrylike trees. The higher she climbed, the nippier the temperature, and she finally had to stop to get a fleece jacket out of her suitcase. The car heater wasn't working too well, and she wanted to keep the window rolled down, anyway, for a better view.

As she had the day before when she started out, she found herself pausing at every opportunity to marvel at the surrounding splendor. From roadside overlooks she could gaze at a panorama of burnished hues as autumn painted its way down the slopes and valleys.

Careful to follow the map Mr. Burkhalter gave her, about ten miles from the town she'd stayed in overnight, she turned onto a gravel road with a sign that read Colton Farms. Beside it was a shield-shaped plaque proudly declaring that a Colton tree had been chosen for the White House a few years back.

She was impressed, not only to know the Coltons produced quality trees, but by the house that suddenly came into view. A white two-story frame with a porch sweeping across the front, it was set back from the road on a commanding hillock. Only a small green square directly in front offered a lawn. Everywhere else, as far as the eye could see, there were rows of trees in different heights and stages of growth.

Jackie thought back to the conversation she'd had with the owner of the motel she stayed in last night. "Ma'am, the Colton family has owned that land as long as I can remember," he'd said. Maybe the family had never let it be known that Roy Colton had left his share to the woman he loved. If so, it made no difference to Jackie. She was the owner now.

No one was in sight, so she continued on to find the pig trail the man at the motel had penciled on the map. It was not too overgrown with weeds, so he was probably right in saying tractors rolled over it every so often. But, unlike the road to the Colton house, the trail had no gravel. There were ruts and holes, and the old car creaked and groaned as she eased her way along.

She figured she had gone perhaps a half mile when the trail crossed a short, rickety-looking plank bridge built over a little rushing stream. The boards bumped in warning as she eased across, and she found herself wondering what would happen after a heavy rain. She might not be able to cross. She could be cut off from the world, and—

Adventure, her mind screamed. It's an adventure, that's all, and adventures never ran smooth. If they did, then they couldn't be called that, could they?

She smiled.

It was going to be all right.

So what if she couldn't cross the bridge for a few days, once in a while. She would make sure to have plenty of supplies, and she'd probably be so busy learning about trees and doing her pottery and writing poetry that she wouldn't even care. Besides, she could always call if she needed anything.

Couldn't she?

She slowed to a bare crawl and stuck her head out the window. Looking around, she didn't see any overhead lines.

Neither were there utility poles.

With a groan she murmured, "Oh, this is just great. No phone. No electricity. And when it rains, I'm stuck."

And you can forget about ordering out for pizza, a little voice inside goaded.

"I didn't come out here to order pizza," she said irritably as she gripped the steering wheel tighter and pressed down on the gas pedal to get the car going again. "I came here for peace and tranquility, and that's what I'm going to have, by God. People that come to the mountains to live have to realize there are certain conveniences they're going to have to give up, and if they can't accept that, then they've no business being here."

The voice needled again. But do they also start talking to themselves?

She gave herself a mental shake. She was being silly. Getting back to nature was what she wanted.

The voice chuckled. *Getting back? You've never been there, girlfriend.* She was a city girl, born and bred.

She clutched the wheel tighter as a tire hit a hole that sent her bouncing up in her seat. Without a belt, she would have hit her head on the roof, and she vowed never to forget to fasten it again. And certainly not on this pig trail of a road.

And then she saw it.

Like a scene from a folksy Norman Rockwell painting, the little log cabin with its quaint porch and rusting tin roof was framed by bright marigolds and leafy hydrangea bushes, thick with pink and blue blossoms. Alongside, curling in and out among the jutting rocks, a tiny stream gurgled its way through ferns and overhanging willow branches. And beyond, an apple orchard, the fruit-laden branches bending precariously toward the ground.

She drew a sharp breath of awe to see a deer nibbling at the apples that had fallen, but then it saw her and, after a mournful stare, turned and bolted back into the forest.

Without realizing it, she had come to a dead stop and was envisioning herself as part of the idyllic setting— sitting on a rock, bare feet dipping into the water, notepad balanced on her knee, she nibbled an apple as she sketched a doe and fawn, and...

Her mouth formed a wide grin and she told herself to get back to reality, for the time being, anyway. There would be time later—and lots of it—for dreaming her life away.

The car coughed its way up the rutted path, and then she was out and running for the cabin Mr. Burkhalter said would be her home now.

She marveled at how well it had been kept up. The logs looked in good condition and appeared to have been recently rechinked. There were a few suspicious planks in the porch floor but nothing in need of immediate attention.

It was small, with only one window on each side of the door. The shutters were closed. She could not see inside.

Taking a deep breath, thrilled to the core to know she was about to enter her new home, she grasped the doorknob and hoped it wasn't locked, because heaven only knew who she would have to see to get a key.

It swung open, and her heart skipped a beat as she took her first step across the threshold.

The furnishings were sparse—a wood table that looked homemade, with benches along two sides, a sofa and chair that had seen better days, but they were positioned before, thank God, a real stone fireplace. That would be her heat, and she could learn to chop wood, by golly, because right then she was so excited she felt as if she could do anything.

She went to the tiny corner kitchen, relieved to see an electric stove. That meant the power lines were underground, so there would be no worry about them falling under ice during the winter.

At the opposite end of the room, she was delighted to find a bedroom, small, but adequate. The double bed with its rusting headboard dominated the room with barely enough room for the old chest of drawers.

And finally, in an alcove, she found the bathroom, with its toilet, a sink with a cracked mirror above and a shower stall.

After inspecting every nook and cranny of the cabin, she ran out to the front porch, and, hugging herself, began turning around and around in her joy till she was so dizzy she practically fell into a cane-backed rocking chair.

Then, eyes misting with tears, she tremulously whispered, "Oh, Libby, if you were here to share it all with me, then it really would be perfect."

She sat there for a long time, rocking back and forth and humming to herself as she gazed at the beauty and serenity all around.

Finally, well aware there was much to be done, she began unloading the car, grateful that bringing the TV and stereo equipment had not been in vain.

The cabin was fairly clean, but she rolled up her sleeves, got a bucket of soapy water and a rag and gave everything a good scrubbing, anyway.

By the time she finished, the sun was low in the sky. Her stomach rumbled with hunger, and that was when she realized that in her excitement and haste, she had not thought about buying groceries. Oh, she had the staples—coffee, sugar, soap and toilet paper. Some bottled water. But she needed food to cook for several days ahead, maybe even weeks.

She had planned to stop by the Colton house and introduce herself, but since she did not know when the grocery stores closed, there might not be time. She could do it on the way back…or the next day.

She would also need to take care of having the electricity changed to her name as soon as she could arrange it. Obviously someone else was paying the bill. Then she began to wonder about that. Just who had been using the cabin? If Libby had known, she probably hadn't cared. But Jackie was curious. She also found herself hoping that whoever it was would not show up in the middle of the night, then decided that was not likely. Though it was being kept up by somebody, it did not appear they had been around lately. The refrigerator had been empty, the temperature on the lowest setting. There were no sheets on the bed, no linens of any kind.

Worrying that the stores would close, she had no time to freshen up. She fluffed her hair again, smoothed her T-shirt, grabbed up her shoulder bag and hurried out to the car in the gathering dusk.

Backing the car out, she caught a glimpse of the peach and watermelon sky over the tops of the pines to the west. She wished she had thought of groceries earlier, so she would not have to make the late trip into town.

It would have been so nice to sit on the porch and sip a glass of wine while watching her first sunset in her new home. But she had not eaten since breakfast and was starting to feel a bit weak and nauseous.

By the time Jackie got to the Piggly-Wiggly on the outskirts she'd had to turn on her headlights. And when she came out a short while later, carrying two plastic bags, it was totally dark.

She breezed through the night, loving the feel of freedom and space and humming to herself all the while. It was going to take some getting used to, being on her own and far removed from the hustle and bustle of life. But she planned to keep busy—very busy. After all, there was much to learn about growing Christmas trees, and—

She had just turned off the main road onto her little dirt pig trail when suddenly one of the tires hit a big rock. The car lurched sharply and came to a jolting stop.

"That's what I get for driving at night," she grumbled as she opened the door and got out to see how much trouble she was really in. She didn't know the road well enough, didn't know all the pitfalls and dangers. But be that as it may, as soon as she could afford it, she planned to have the road properly graded, gravel put down so there wouldn't be so many potholes, and—

Slapping a hand against her forehead she groaned out loud.

From the glow of the taillight she could see that she was stuck in a rut up to her hubcap, and it was going to be extremely hard to pull out of it.

She got back behind the steering wheel, pressed the accelerator, then realized the tire was spinning and she was only getting in deeper.

Adding to her woes was the knowledge she hadn't thought to bring a flashlight. It was probably a mile or more to the cabin, but if she managed to keep on the road she could make it in the dark. The thing to do, however, was hurry before it got any later. Then the critters would be roaming about, and she didn't want to encounter any bears.

Gathering up the two plastic bags, she realized how heavy they were. If she left the canned goods behind, she could easily carry the perishables.

She began unpacking the sacks, sorting by the feel of things what to take with her.

Leaning inside, her head between the seats, she did not see or hear the truck until it stopped directly behind her. Whirling about, she found herself blinded by the lights and quickly dropped the bags and dove into the front seat. Maybe it was a neighbor offering help, but she was taking no chances and rolled up the windows and locked the doors.

Clutching the steering wheel, she sank down in the seat as far as she could, willing herself invisible as she heard the truck's engine turn off, a door open and close and then the solemn crunch of footsteps coming toward her. The beam of a flashlight shone directly in her face as a masculine voice boomed in the stillness, "Are you all right in there?"

She nodded, eyes squeezed shut against the glare. Lifting one hand from the steering wheel she waved in protest. "Please. I can't see."

He dropped the beam from her face to shine it around inside. "There's no need for you to be afraid, miss. I see you're stuck, and I'll help you get out, but would you mind telling me what you're doing out here this time of night?"

She kept her grip on the steering wheel as though it were a weapon. "I'm on my way home. I wasn't used to this...this pig trail, and I'm afraid I let my tires slip out of the ruts and into some soft dirt."

He laughed in surprise. "Ma'am, nobody lives down this road. You must be really turned around. Now where were you headed? I don't recollect seeing you or your car in these parts, and believe me, I know everybody for miles around."

"I told you," she said defensively, "I'm on my way home. I live down this road—not that you can call it a road," she added waspishly.

He tapped on the window with his flashlight. "Ma'am, would you please roll it down so we can talk? You're lost and don't realize it."

She decided he did not sound like a serial killer. In fact, he had a very nice voice—warm, husky, and nothing about him had thus far given her reason to be wary. Still, she was alone and miles from civilization, so she cranked the window down only a few inches. "I'm not lost. I moved in earlier today and went into town for groceries. I made sure I took all the right turns, so if you'll just give me a push, I'll thank you and be on my way."

He gave an exasperated sigh. "I'll give you a push but not to send you on down this road, because you've got no business there."

She decided it best not to argue further, at least not while one of her tires was buried to the hubcap. She made her voice light and sweet and very grateful. "Maybe you're right. Maybe I am turned around. I'll just go back to town and start over."

"Whatever. Just don't keep going in that direction. You're on private property."

She knew that, because it was her private property, which he would find out sooner or later. Probably he was a hunter, used to going and coming on Libby's land anytime he felt like it, because, till now, there had been no one to protest. But it was late, and all she wanted was to go home and have that glass of wine on the porch she had promised herself. "Sure. Just give me a push."

"It's not that easy. Looks like you spun your wheels to try and get out and wound up in deeper. I'll have to use the winch."

She had no idea what a winch was but soon found out when she watched in the truck's beams as he attached a thick black cable and hook to the rear of her car. Then he eased the truck back to pull her free.

After he took the cable off, she started the engine and continued driving in the direction she had been going. He would think she was going to find a place to turn around. Already in the rearview mirror she could see he had turned around, but he wouldn't expect her to try it without four-wheel drive. By the time he realized she was not following behind him, she would be safely inside the cabin with the door locked.

She wondered what to do about a phone. There were no lines that she could see, no evidence of any jacks inside. Maybe there was a cell tower perched on a mountaintop somewhere nearby that would give a signal strong enough for her to have that kind of phone.

Deep in thought, excited over everything in her life for the first time in too long to remember, she did not notice headlights coming up behind her. But when she did, she was ready to turn in the driveway, and by the time the stranger's truck pulled in, she was running up the porch steps.

"Wait, hold it right there." He was out of the truck

and rushing to follow. "I hate to call the sheriff on you, ma'am, but I will if you don't stop."

She was at the door, hand on the knob. The groceries were still in the car. She hadn't stopped to get them, anxious to get inside to safety. "Call him," she yelled over her shoulder. "He can't stop me from going in my own home, and neither can you."

She slammed the door and locked it.

"Are you crazy?" He pounded on the door. "Who the hell are you?"

She went to the open window to crisply inform him, "I am the new owner of this property. My name is Jackie Lundigan."

Instantly indignant, he cried, "That can't be true. I would have heard about if Libby Pratt had sold this place. And she'd never do that, anyway."

Jackie leaned so that she could see him in the porch light she had switched on. He had a nice face, but at the moment it was a very angry face. "Did you know Libby?"

"I've never met her, but I know enough about her to believe she'd never sell, and—" he paused "—wait a minute. You asked if I knew her. What is that supposed to mean?"

Jackie swallowed hard, hating to put it in words. "She's dead. She died a few weeks ago."

"Well, I'm sorry," he said, genuinely sounding as though he were. "But that doesn't explain your marching in and claiming this place as yours."

"I have papers to prove it."

"Then let's see them."

She stiffened. "I don't think it's any of your business."

"Well, I'd say it most definitely is, since I happen to own all the land around here. My name's Colton. Sam Colton."

Chapter Four

Jackie darted quick glances out the window as she finished whipping eggs and cream for cheese blintzes.

Butter sizzled in the skillet. Coffee was brewing. The table was set, and she had picked a bouquet of marigolds to go in the center.

Everything looked nice and, most of all, friendly, which was the atmosphere she wanted when Sam Colton arrived.

During their hapless encounter of the night before, she had produced her copy of the deed. Afraid to open the door for fear he might yank it out of her hand, she had shown it to him through the window. While he had remained unconvinced of her right to be there, at least he had capitulated enough that he had not called the sheriff on his CB. That would have been an unnecessary embarrassment for them both, not to mention the inconvenience for the sheriff.

It had been her suggestion that they continue the discussion this morning, and he had grudgingly agreed.

In the scant light she been unable to distinguish much about him except that he was tall and had a voice that crazily made her think of hot chocolate and marshmallows.

She guessed him to be thirtyish and thought she'd caught a glimpse of blue eyes but told herself she wasn't supposed to be interested in his looks. All she wanted was his cooperation in helping her learn all she needed to know to take an active part in her share of the tree farm. So she did not want to alienate him, if at all possible.

Earlier, at the first light of dawn, she had gone out to pick the marigolds and taken time to walk up and down the rows of fragrant trees, savoring every breath she drew. It had been a magical time as she dared think she might actually be embarking on her true destiny in life, that all the hurts of the past had merely been stepping stones to peace, contentment, and—

Gravel crunched, and she looked up from the stove to see a red truck. She had not noticed the color of Sam Colton's the night before but knew it could only be him.

He eased to a stop, was taking his time getting out. A good sign. It meant he wasn't in a rush for an angry confrontation.

By the time he walked up the steps, she was at the door to offer what she hoped was a dazzling smile. "Good morning. I hope Mrs. Colton didn't fix too big a breakfast for you. I make a mean cheese blintz and would love for you to try one."

"There is no Mrs. Colton," he said curtly, coldly. "And I never eat breakfast."

So he wasn't married. Reminding herself not to care,

she quickly said, "Well you should, you know. Breakfast is the most important meal of the day."

His sharp glance told her he thought she was out of line.

She shrugged in apology. "I'm a dietician. Meddling with other people's diets is what I do."

"Well, please don't meddle with mine." He glanced about. "Looks like you've made yourself right at home."

It was her turn to be curt. "Mr. Colton, I am at home." Then, to soften, added, "Has someone else been living here? Everything seemed so well cared for."

"I had cause to live here for a little while. I didn't think Miss Pratt would mind. The place had been closed up for years. I just left it open after I moved out, thinking a worker and his family might want to use it one day, but so far that hasn't happened."

"Well, I'll be keeping it up from now on. I intend to live here permanently."

He frowned. "There's a lot to be resolved here."

She was right. He did have blue eyes. And his hair was the color of corn shucks, and as wild and unruly as the silks blowing in the wind.

With a mental shake to toss off such thoughts, she retorted, "Not really. I showed you the paper last night that the court issued pending probate of Libby's will. The attorney said it was all the proof of ownership I need, and—"

He cut her off. "And I don't care what the attorney said. Nobody has told me anything. I didn't even know Miss Pratt had died."

"I imagine Mr. Burkhalter—he's the attorney handling her estate—will be sending you a letter as soon as he gets around to it. He said it will take about six months to settle her estate, and—''

''Please spare me the details. If you're telling the truth, I'll hear them sooner or later. Who are you, anyway? A relative of hers, I suppose.''

She did not like his attitude one little bit, and he seemed to be growing more hostile by the minute. ''No, we weren't kin to each other,'' she said, ''but we were very close. My name is Jackie Lundigan, and I'm afraid you're going to have to hear the details, since I'm the new owner.''

He quirked a brow. ''That's what you say. The fact is, Libby Pratt never had any right to this land in the first place. I suppose you know how she happened to come by it?''

''I do. Roy Colton willed it to her before he was killed.''

''Yes, because he was going off to war and fancied himself in love with her. And it's understandable how he could do something so impulsive. The part that is not understandable—and what my family could never accept—was her not seeing it that way and giving the land back. She had no right to it. She and Uncle Roy were never married. They were just teenagers. And if he'd had time to think about it, he never would have done it.''

''Well, if your family objected so strongly, why didn't they challenge Roy's will? Who would have owned the land then, anyway? Your great-grandfather?''

His frown deepened. ''He was already dead, and the land had been divided between my father and Uncle Roy. There was nothing anybody could do—except Libby, who should have signed it back over to the Colton family, like I said. Only she didn't.''

He shook his head solemnly from side to side, then

concluded, "No, Miss Lundigan. Libby Pratt had no right to this land, but at least she had the good sense to stay off it. She collected the money and left me alone. Now here you come, an intruder, all set to take over. It isn't right."

Jackie put her hands on her hips and cocked her head and looked him straight in the eye. She had to raise her chin, because he was several inches taller than she was. She could smell butter burning and knew the blintzes were probably ruined but no longer cared. A nice get-acquainted breakfast between neighbors and business partners had suddenly turned ugly.

It was all she could do to keep from wagging her finger in his face as she challenged, "Did it ever occur to you, Mr. Colton, that Libby Pratt kept this land because it was all she had left of the man she loved so much she could never love another? This land, and—" she rushed to the kitchen windowsill where she had placed the little carved rolling pin "—this." She held it up for him to see. "He made it for her, and she treasured it almost as much as a wedding band."

He started to speak, but she rushed to continue, not giving him a chance. "And there's something else I think we better get straight from the get-go, Mr. Colton, and that's your remark about me being all set to take over. The fact is, I'm not set at all. I don't know the first thing about growing Christmas trees, and I would be most grateful if you would teach me all I need to know. However, if you have a problem with that and continue your arrogance and resentment for me—as well as the memory of a woman I couldn't have loved more if she'd been blood kin—then I think I'd best get busy and hire someone else to work my half of this farm."

He looked her up and down with incredulity.

"You...you can't do that," he sputtered. "The Colton family has operated this farm since right after the Civil War, when Christmas trees started being sold commercially."

"Then think about that," she said, a bit sharper than intended. It had to be quite a shock for him, so she softly added, "Look. I don't want a land war here, Mr. Colton. I want us to be friends and partners if that's possible. Now why don't you let me fix a new batch of blintzes?" She wrinkled her nose and smiled. "I think the others are a lost cause. Then we can talk this out and get to know each other."

"I don't need to get to know you, Miss Lundigan, because this isn't going to work at all."

"Then I take it you want me to start looking for someone to oversee my share of the farm till I learn how to run things myself?"

His eyes narrowed. "What's the name of that lawyer again? I think I'd better call him and get this straightened out."

She crossed to where she had left her purse and dug around till she found Mr. Burkhalter's card, then handed it to him. "There's really nothing to straighten out, but I'm sure he'll be glad to verify everything I've told you."

He stared at the card, tight-lipped and grim, then stuffed it in the pocket of his faded denim shirt. "It isn't right. She should have given it back to the family."

"If you think about it, Mr. Colton, you might understand. It was all she had left of him and the love they shared. Except for the little rolling pin," she added. "Now about those blintzes." She forced another perky smile. "If you'll try one, I promise you'll change your mind about not wanting to eat breakfast."

"No, thanks."

He turned to go, and she was right behind him.

"Wait. Please. I have so many questions to ask you. Can't you stay for just a cup of coffee?"

He whirled on her, his glare withering. "Till I talk to this lawyer, I can't see where you and I have anything to discuss, Miss Lundigan."

"Yes, we do," she said, ire rising as she followed him down the porch steps. "For one thing you can stop calling me Miss Lundigan. Call me Jackie, please. And I'd like to call you Sam, because, like it or not, we are partners—for the time being, anyway."

Again he turned on her. "I want to ask you something. Just exactly where are you from?"

She told him.

"Durham, North Carolina," he scoffed. "That's in the flatlands. Have you always lived there?"

She nodded, wondering where he was going with his inquisition. She could see the corners of his mouth twitching.

"And how much time have you spent in the mountains?"

She thought a moment. "Not much. A trip or two when I was a kid. But I already know I'm going to love it." She swung her arms. "Who wouldn't? It's gorgeous here."

"Not all the time. Have you ever been here in the winter?"

"No, but—"

"It gets cold. Real cold. It freezes. We have snowstorms when the snow gets so deep it's almost up to the roof of this cabin. Why do you think there are so many ski lodges around? Because we have snow."

"I like snow," she crisply informed him. "It's pretty."

"For a time, yes, but not when you have to get out and work in it. If there's ice, it has to be shaken off the limbs of the young trees so they won't break. There's danger of frostbite if you aren't careful, and it's unbelievably cold."

She shrugged. "So I'll layer."

"You're trying to be smart, Miss Lundigan—Jackie— and that's your first mistake—thinking mountain living is right out of a picture book. You won't make it through the first winter. And the weather isn't the only thing you have to worry about. We have critters here—bears, timber rattlers, a panther once in a while. You can't venture out at night without a gun." He smirked. "And you don't look like the gun-totin' kind to me."

She went stiff from head to toe, and her hands clenched into fists at her sides as she silently commanded herself to respond, not react and let him make her lose control and look foolish. "I can learn to tote a gun, as you call it. I can also learn everything I need to know to survive. I'm not a wimp."

He took her by surprise, his hand snaking out to grab one of hers and hold it up to pry open, revealing her palm. "Nice manicure, lady. Nails all smooth and polished. No sap stains from the trees. No splinters. No calluses. Just a tender little hand that makes cheese blintzes. So I take back what I said about you not lasting the first winter. Hell, you won't make through the first ice storm."

He turned on his heel and walked away, and she felt like snatching up a rock to throw at his retreating back, but thought better of it. Who did he think he was?

She watched, quaking with fury, as he started backing

the red truck out of the driveway. Then, seeing the gun rack in the back of his cab, she cried, "Wait…" and ran down the steps.

He did not try to hide his irritation as he leaned out the window. "Look, there's no need arguing about this. I'm going to call the lawyer and see if there's some way we can settle this. If it's like you say it is, then we have to talk about me buying you out. It's ridiculous for you to even think about staying."

"You don't have enough money to buy me out," she said, then pointed at the gun rack. "But we need to get something settled right away. There will be no hunting on my land. A man in town told me how he and others hunt here, and I won't allow it."

Again, his expression was one of absolute amazement. "You can't stop it. Folks have been hunting these mountains for generations—bear, deer, turkey."

"And I suppose you're one of them?"

"No. I've never cared for hunting."

"Well, that's in your favor," she acknowledged. "But you can tell your friends they won't be hunting on this land anymore."

Their eyes met and held in challenge, and finally Sam was the first to speak, ice dripping from his tone. "Well, first we've got to make sure it is your land, and then you can start making rules. Till then, I advise you to tread lightly. The locals don't take kindly to newcomers trying to change their ways."

Frost was also in her voice as she fired back, hands on her hips, "Well, they'd better get use to it where I'm concerned, Sam Colton, because, like it or not, I'm here to stay."

He gave her a long look, then smiled to say, "I take

back what I said about you not making it through the first winter.''

She felt a rush of satisfaction to think she had been able to change his mind about her so fast, but the feeling quickly faded at his next words.

''You won't make it till Christmas.''

Sam spun gravel, backing out of the driveway and felt foolish afterward. That's what a kid would do, and he was no kid. He knew about life and farming and Christmas trees, and most of all, he knew about selfish, headstrong women like Jackie Lundigan.

No matter that she was cuter than a speckled pup and had green eyes as big as saucers and hair the color of the September sun over the Blue Ridge on an autumn afternoon. And maybe he had felt a stirring at how her high, round bottom filled out her tight jeans and the way her breasts pushed at the T-shirt she was wearing. None of that mattered. She was a city girl, a flatlander, and she had no business here. Besides, he had enough problems without having to deal with her.

The family hadn't liked it one little bit that his uncle Roy had left his share of the farm to Libby Pratt. But at least she had kept her distance, never trying to interfere with any of the operations. She had taken the money she was sent and never asked questions. Sam knew it would have been really easy to cheat her, but his family took pride in being honest. She always got what she had coming to her. They had been fair, so, dammit, why couldn't she have seen the fairness in giving the land back when she died? What right did she have to leave it to someone who wasn't even her kin, for Pete's sake?

And who was this Jackie Lundigan, anyway, and how did she wind up being Libby Pratt's heir?

He drove back to the house, took the front porch steps two at a time, hurried to his office and snatched up the phone. He dialed the number on the card, and on the second ring a woman answered to crisply announce, "Mr. Burkhalter's office."

At first she said he was unavailable, but Sam persisted. Finally she put him through, and Mr. Burkhalter politely confirmed that yes, Jackie Lundigan was the new owner of the property formerly held by Miss Libby Pratt, and if Sam needed written proof, it would be no problem.

"Okay, okay, I believe you," Sam said, hating to admit it. "But none of this makes any sense. Libby Pratt had no family, and mine—before they died out—figured she was only hanging on to the land for sentimental reasons. We always thought—hoped—she had made provisions to turn it back over to us when she passed away rather than leave it to strangers."

"Ms. Lundigan was hardly a stranger to Miss Pratt. She was quite fond of her. Every time I visited her at the nursing home, she talked about how good she was to her...how she was the granddaughter she never had."

Something clicked, and Sam cried, "Wait a minute. You're saying Miss Pratt was in a nursing home?"

"Yes. Unfortunately she was in an accident right after she retired. Such a shame. She had so many plans."

"So she met Jackie Lundigan in the nursing home?"

"That's right. She was the dietician there. They became very close."

"So it would seem," Sam said under his breath, then, edgily, concluded, "well, I guess there's nothing to be done."

"Except that you two will hopefully become good friends," Mr. Burkhalter said cheerfully. "Jackie is really a nice lady, and she's so enthusiastic about making a new life up there in those beautiful mountains. I'm sure once you get to know her, the two of you will get along splendidly.

"Now then," he added in a rush, "I've got to get to court, but I'll have my secretary send you some documents to put your mind at ease."

"No, that's all right. I'm sure everything is legal. Thank you for your time."

Sam hung up and clenched the phone so tightly his knuckles turned white.

So that's how it was.

Another female who couldn't be trusted.

Thinking how Jackie Lundigan had cozied up to an old lady, to get her to leave her everything she had, turned his stomach. And feeling as he did, how the hell was he going to be able to accept her as a business partner?

And what was her motive, anyway? Why had she left the excitement and convenience of the city to move to the rugged mountains and bad winter weather? Why hadn't she just stayed where she was and collected her share of the money like Libby Pratt had done?

There was something strange about her, and he intended to find out what it was.

He also intended to try his best to get rid of her.

In town the first person Sam ran into was Deputy Earl Whaley.

"Did that woman find you, that was looking for your farm last night?"

It was a small town, and soon it would be all over that Libby Pratt's heir had arrived. And the thing was, his family had kept it a secret all these years that Roy had left his share to her. The locals would have a field day with this juicy tidbit, for sure, but they weren't going to hear anything from him.

"Yeah, she did," he said, starting to move on by. He was heading for the hardware store to buy more rope. When tree harvest began in a few weeks, he would need plenty for bundling. Tom Haskins, the owner, always ordered a mammoth order just for him.

"She acted a little strange," Earl said, scratching his chin to think about it. "I helped her out. Showed her to a motel here. What was funny, though, was how she was up there with a map and said she was checking on things for the owner."

Sam was about to push the door to the hardware store open but froze. "She said *what?*"

Earl repeated himself, then added, "She also gave the impression that she had thought the owner was a woman, and she was checking on things for her."

Sam uttered an oath and pushed on inside. Exactly what was she up to, talking like Libby Pratt was still alive?

"She's a pretty thing," Earl called after him. "I wish she'd been looking for my land."

Earl's laugh grated on his ears, and Sam went inside. He was cursing himself up and down for letting things go this far. Years ago, when his father died, he had thought about going to see Libby to get her to sell him her portion. Since she hadn't done anything with it in over fifty years, he thought there might be a chance she'd be willing to give it up, seeing as how she was getting on up there herself. But he had never got around to it, because things started going sour with Donna along about then.

"Sam Colton. You're just the man I want to see."

Sam was almost at the counter when he heard Willa Kearney as she came in the door after him.

He groaned inwardly. All gossip eventually passed through the Book Nook, and Willa took it upon herself to see that it spread beyond.

"There was a young woman in the store yesterday with an old map of your land. Seemed surprised when Eddie told her you owned the whole thing. She gave him the impression she thought you didn't."

She could only mean Eddie Parks, who carried tales worse than Willa because he covered more territory working his magazine route. "What kind of old map?"

"An old one apparently. It showed the part your Uncle Roy would've got if he'd lived. Everybody knows it was divided up that way, once upon a time. I remember clear as a bell." A nostalgic expression took over her wrinkled face. "Your great-grandaddy came into my pa's store, proud as punch because he'd had a map professionally drawn by a real surveyor. I was only around ten at the time. I heard him tell my pa how he had cut the land in two for his boys.

"But that was before he died," she added with sadness, "and before the war took your great-uncle."

"I know." Sam tried not to sound impatient. He had heard the story all his life. His great-grandfather had been willing to divide the land between his sons before he died, all right, but had probably rolled over in his grave if he knew what Roy had done with his share.

Willa persisted. "So who was that woman, and where did she get that old map?"

Sam did not like lying and made it a habit not to, but until he had a chance to persuade Jackie Lundigan into selling him her share, he did not want word to spread.

"I have no idea," he fibbed. "But I'll let you know if I see her."

"Well, she headed out that way right after Eddie pointed the way. You didn't see her? That's strange."

Mercifully, Tom came out of the storage room to see Sam and tell him his rope had arrived. "Don't think you can get the whole order in your truck at one time, though."

Sam was able to smile, despite feeling so low. "Haven't been able to in twelve years, Tom. No need to think I can now. I'll just have to make several trips during the next week."

Willa was leaning against the counter, tapping a finger to her nose as though in deep thought. "Maybe you ought to look off the mountain on them sharp curves, Sam. She could've run off, not being used to driving around here."

Tom looked from one to the other. "Who ran off the road? Who are y'all talking about?"

Sam hurriedly gathered up the bundles of rope.

When he didn't answer Tom's questions, Willa did not hesitate to do so herself. "Some woman was looking for Sam yesterday—or for his farm, that is. She had a real old map. I think it was a copy of the one Ben Colton had made up back in the forties."

"I'll take this on out," Sam called over his shoulder, heading for the door and leaving them to speculate about the strange woman who had come to town.

When he was gone, Tom leaned across the counter, interest piqued, to ask Willa, "What's this all about? Sam acted like he was worried about something."

Willa likewise leaned closer. "If you ask me, I think he's already come upon that woman, and something hap-

pened that's got him upset. I know Sam. Known him all
his life. And I can tell when something's got him
stirred.''

"So what do you suppose?" Tom scowled. "You
don't suppose it's got anything to do with Donna, do
you? I tell you, that woman should be ashamed of what
she did to him.''

"True. But he's better off without her, especially
when she turned out the way she did. If he's smart, he'll
marry one of his own kind next time and not some city
girl who'll never get used to living here. That was
Donna's problem, that and the fact she had the morals
of an alley cat.''

Tom made a clucking sound and wagged his finger.
"Now, now, Willa. We don't know the whole story
about what happened there.''

Willa snorted. "I know all I need to. She was a little
tramp, that's what, and now I'm wondering about this
one looking for him yesterday. Maybe she's a friend of
Donna's, come to see if she can get some money out of
him.''

Willa turned so she could watch Sam through the window as he loaded the rope onto the back of his truck.

"I'll tell you one thing, though," she said, almost
angrily, "I'll do everything I can to keep the same thing
from happening again. So if that little gal yesterday is
up to no good, I hope she kept right on going.''

Sam came back in for the rest of the rope.

Willa boldly asked, "So how do you think she got
her hands on that old map, Sam?''

"I have no idea," he responded woodenly.

"If I run into her, I'll see if I can find out.''

Sam did not respond as he picked up the rope and
hurried to get out of there. Willa would, he knew, even-

tually find out how Jackie Lundigan came in possession of the map to his great-uncle's land.

But he intended to find out much more—like how she was able to get Libby Pratt to will it to her.

Chapter Five

Nearly a week had passed since Jackie had the encounter with Sam Colton, and she had seen nothing of him since. It suited her just fine. She was busy fixing up the cabin to her tastes, as well as familiarizing herself with the woods immediately around her.

The trees around her were not very tall. Maybe three feet. She still enjoyed walking in the rows between. The smell was exhilarating, but then, so was everything around her. She loved the sunrises, the sunsets, and the beautiful day in between.

So far, she had seen nothing to be afraid of. There was no lock on the front door, however, and she resolved the next time she went into town she would buy one and try to install it herself.

And she would need to go into town soon, she thought that morning as she walked around the little clearing that was her yard. She was nearly out of staples, and she needed a few art supplies. She also wanted to ask the location of the nearest nursing home so she could start visiting. Sadly there were always residents who either had no family or whose relatives were too far away to come often.

She had gathered apples from the trees beside the cabin and, after ruining a few pies as she learned to operate the old stove, had finally produced what she thought was worthy of a county fair blue ribbon.

Smelling deliciously of butter and cinnamon, she placed it on the kitchen windowsill to cool, then went outside to sit on the lawn and look for four-leaf clovers.

With the azure sky a canopy above and plump, fat clouds drifting overhead to provide shade now and then from the warm autumn sun, Jackie acknowledged that even though she was enjoying herself, it would soon be time to get serious. She had heard chain saws buzzing in the distance the day before and knew the Christmas tree harvesting had begun. She wanted to see it, be a part of it, and that meant contacting Sam Colton and she wasn't sure how to go about it. She hated to just boldly walk right up and knock on his front door and inform him she was there to start working with him. But she saw no other way.

Actually, she thought it rude and very unneighborly that he hadn't been back to see her. He would have called Mr. Burkhalter by now, of course, so he knew she was telling the truth about everything. So why hadn't he returned? After all, whether he liked it or not, they were now business partners, and they were going to have to communicate with each other.

A movement among the brush at the edge of the forest caught her eye.

She sat up straight, invisible tendrils of fear twining

about her body. She knew enough about nature to fear it might be a bear, searching for mast to stoke his—or her—big body with fuel for the long hibernating months ahead when winter arrived. The nights had been very cool lately, and she'd had to dig a blanket out of a trunk, but it was still too warm to cause the animals to bed down for the season, so she was quite wary.

Bears, she had heard, could get up to speeds of nearly thirty-five miles an hour in an open field, but this was no open field. Still, she would have to sprint to make it to the cabin in time. And then what?

"Stop it, you wimp," she said out loud. "Or you're going to make Sam Colton's prediction come true."

At that, the leaves moved again, and she thought she caught a glimpse of red.

Bears weren't red.

A fox?

But it was too bright for a fox.

Now the tendrils of fear tightened as she realized it might be a two-legged animal out there...a man.

Slowly she got to her feet, pretending to be oblivious to anything around her. She began sauntering slowly toward the cabin, looking down at the ground as though still in search of four-leaf clovers. But her heart was pounding like crazy, and she resolved, then and there, that when she went into town she would buy a gun. Out here in the wilderness and all alone, like it or not, she needed protection. Sad, but that was the reality in the world we live in, she thought, inching her way along, waiting for the right second to break and run.

She would sling a chair in front of the door, then run to the kitchen for a knife and scream her head off, and...

She froze.

The bushes were no longer rustling behind her, but

beside her instead, and she laughed to see a brilliant red cardinal perched on a limb nearby.

"So you're the red monster I saw creeping in the woods," she said to him, feeling a bit foolish to have allowed herself to be so scared. She had to get over that. She could not, by golly, panic at each little sound. After all, the woods were full of noises if one only listened.

The cardinal cocked his head and stared at her, probably bemused over having a human speak to him for the first time in his life. As though deciding the experience too unnerving, he flew away.

"So much for your company," Jackie said, continuing on to the cabin. Maybe she should buy a bird feeder when she went to town.

Suddenly, going into town seemed a major priority. There was so much she needed, and it was time to get busy and stop playing nature girl.

Right then, however, she wanted a slice of the apple pie while it was still warm, and a cup of the delicious coffee she had brewed earlier in the old blue enamel pot.

The coffee was still warm. She wished for fresh cream but had not thought to buy any and had to use the powdered kind instead.

Picking up a slicing knife, she started for the windowsill. "And now to taste a real apple pie— What?" She gasped.

The sill was empty.

The pie was gone.

"I don't believe this. Pesky raccoons." She set the knife aside and marched to the front door, down the steps, and around the corner. They had raided the garbage can two nights before, and while she enjoyed watching them from the glow of the back porch light, she had made it a point to leave all trash inside till time to take it into town for disposal.

Stealing a pie, however, was beyond the limits of her tolerance for cute wildlife. She had worked hard, and besides, they weren't supposed to be out during daylight hours, anyway.

She spotted the pie sitting on the ground and was puzzled to see that only one portion had been very neatly scooped out. Raccoons didn't eat that way. No animal did.

What then?

Glancing all about, she was overcome with the creepy feeling that someone was watching her. Could it be one of the Colton farm workers who had strayed away from the work area, lured by the smell of homemade apple pie?

Mustering bravado, she called, "All right. Whoever you are, come out of there and face the music. If you wanted a slice of pie, all you had to do was ask. You didn't have to steal it."

There was no response.

She bent down and picked up the remainder of the pie. "All right. Be a coward about it. But I won't put any more pies on the sill to cool. You can be sure of that. Not with a thief around."

There was only the slightest rustling in the brush but it was enough to tell her where the culprit was hiding. "I know you're in there. Now come on out and introduce yourself. I'm not mad, really. And it gets lonely out here. I wouldn't mind making a friend."

She began backing toward the cabin, feeling a bit uneasy. She had extended an invitation to forgive and forget, yet they would not come forth. So maybe it wasn't an innocent case of pie stealing, at all. Maybe it was someone hiding in the woods and up to no good, an escaped convict, perhaps. Was there even a prison close by? She had no idea.

Now she felt stupid for having acted so nonchalant about it all. What she should have done was jump in the car and drive away. But one thing was for certain, before the sun went down she would have a good, solid lock on the front door, as well as all the windows.

Maybe she would buy a CB, too, to have communication with the outside world. While it seemed like a lark at first, with terror inching up her spine, she now realized the folly of being so cut off from everything.

She made it around the corner of the cabin, then, resisting the urge to just bolt inside, grab the car keys and get out of there, she paused.

She put the pie on the porch railing, then went back to press against the chinked logs and inch her way back just far enough that she could peek toward the rear of the yard again.

And then she saw him.

A little boy who looked to be around five or six years old had stepped out of the bushes and was slinking toward the rows of Christmas trees.

Smiling, and filled with wonder over the pint-size pie thief, Jackie quietly moved to follow after him.

Intent on reaching the haven of the forest, the boy was unaware of her presence...until she sprang forward to clamp both hands on his shoulders and cry, "Gotcha!"

To her amazement, he did not scream, nor attempt to make any kind of sound. Neither did he struggle. Instead his knees buckled and he fell to the ground to stare up at her with wide, tear-filled eyes.

At once Jackie dropped beside him. "Hey, little bandit, I'm sorry. I shouldn't have scared you like that. And taking the pie is no big deal, really. I'm not mad, and there's no cause for you to be afraid.''

He continued to stare at her, eyes still round with fear.

She reached for his hands, which were sticky with pie juice. She could feel him trembling. ''Please, don't be frightened. I'm not going to hurt you.''

His expression said he wasn't so sure of that.

''What's your name?''

Silence.

''Mine's Jackie.'' She gave him what she hoped was a reassuring smile. ''Tell you what—it's damp here on the ground. Why don't we go back to my cabin and have some milk and another slice of pie? This time on a plate with a fork, so it won't be so messy.''

He shook his head.

''Tummy full? Then how about a glass of milk to wash it down?'' Then she remembered she'd finished off the bottle that morning with her oatmeal. ''Oops. Sorry. Fresh out of milk. But I've got some soda. What do you say?''

She thought she caught a glimmer of interest. Standing, she gently pulled him up with her. ''Come on. Let's get acquainted.''

He held back.

''I won't hurt you. I promise. I want to be your friend, little guy.''

She could feel his reluctance as he shuffled along beside her, her arm around his little shoulders. He was a cute little boy with a sprinkling of freckles on the tip of his nose. But she was struck by his lackluster brown eyes and his overall somber mood. Maybe he was just embarrassed over having been caught and worried she would tell his parents.

"I won't tell," she said suddenly, brightly, as they reached the porch. "It wasn't right to steal, though. I'm sure you know that. But we'll just forget it happened, and the next time you want a slice of pie or a cookie or whatever, you just knock on my door, and I'll fix you right up, okay?"

She patted him and bent down to see his face, expecting some kind of reaction—relief, joy, whatever. But there was nothing. He just continued to stare at her dully.

She sighed. He was a strange little boy. He also looked a bit unkempt. His hair could use trimming, and the knees of his jeans were worn and needed mending. His sneakers were untied, but she fixed those right away, tying a bow on each.

"Won't you even tell me your name?" she pleaded.

He cast a wistful glance at the pie, still sitting on the porch railing.

She did not miss it and cried, "Aha! You are still hungry. Well, then, my mysterious friend, we will swap a name for a slice of pie. Come on."

He followed her inside and, without being told, climbed up on the bench beside the table.

Cutting a large wedge of pie, Jackie put it on a plate, then, along with a napkin and fork, placed it before him. "I wish I had ice cream to go on top, but I forgot to buy any. I'm going into town today, and I'll get some for your next visit. How's that?"

He started eating.

She sat down on the bench opposite and watched him, eyes narrowed as she wondered what was going on here. Then it dawned, and she could have kicked herself for not realizing it before. The boy was a mute. That explained why he did not answer when she had first called out to him. He could not hear a word she said.

"You're deaf, aren't you?" she said softly, resisting the impulse to reach out and run her fingertips down his soft cheek in sympathy.

But suddenly he looked at her and shook his head, and she was so startled she almost fell backward off the bench. "You hear," she yelped.

He nodded.

"Then why won't you talk to me?"

He dropped his eyes to the pie and continued shoveling huge bites into his mouth.

Maybe, she decided, he was just shy. "Well, maybe you'll talk to me when you get to know me a little better. You will come back to see me, won't you?"

Still he did not speak, and when he finished his pie, he politely wiped his mouth with the paper napkin, then got down off the bench and walked toward the door.

Jackie was right behind him.

"I can't let you just leave like this, little bandit—and that's a good name till you tell me your real one. You could get hurt out there traipsing through those woods. Snakes and bears and no telling what else. Now you just wait here and let me get my car keys, and I'll drive you home. If you don't want to talk, you can point me in the right direction."

With a pat on his head, she hurried into the bedroom where she had left her purse and keys.

And when she returned, he was gone.

Jackie saw no sign of Sam as she passed his house on her way to town. She wondered where he was working…where trees were being harvested and if it was even time. She had heard chain saws, all right, but that might not mean anything. Actually she was frustrated not to know beans about growing Christmas trees, anyway. The only thing she knew was that around the end of November she started seeing them for sale in front of grocery stores or in vacant lots.

That had to change, she thought with firm resolve as she turned onto Main Street. And the place to start was reading, which meant a visit to Willa Kearney's Book Nook.

But first things first.

At a corner gas station she spotted a pay phone inside the door and pulled in. With a long-distance card, she called Mr. Burkhalter's office, but his secretary said he was in court.

"Well, maybe you can help me," Jackie persisted. "Do you know whether a man named Sam Colton called him to verify my inheritance?"

"He must have," his secretary said. "Mr. Burkhalter had me send him some papers to do just that. Is there a problem, something you want me to tell Mr. Burkhalter about?"

"I hope not. Thanks."

So that's how it was going to be, she mused as she got on with her shopping. By now Sam would have received everything he needed to prove she was telling the truth, but he was obviously taking the attitude that it didn't mean anything. He was just going to ignore her. Well, she had news for him.

After buying groceries, she crossed the street to the Book Nook.

The instant she opened the door she could smell good things baking and fresh coffee brewing.

Glancing about, she was grateful there were no other customers.

Willa was rearranging a display of greeting cards and smiled to see her. "I remember you. You were in here about a week or so ago, asking Eddie about the Colton place. Did you find it?''

Jackie knew there was going to be no getting around being the target of prying questions. After all, it was a small town, and a newcomer was, no doubt, big news. ''Yes, I did, thank you.'' Then, to hedge, she asked, ''Do you have any reference books?''

Immediately Willa's brow furrowed as she looked her up and down. ''What kind of reference books? I hope you don't mean sex books. I don't carry stuff like that.'' She winked. ''But I do carry lots of romance novels. You won't believe how many I sell. And believe me, that's all you need to feel all cuddly and loving, and—''

Jackie swallowed a groan and moved to cut her off lest she keep hurtling down the wrong track. ''No ma'am. Nothing like that. I'm interested in books on Christmas trees…how to grow them.''

Curtly Willa demanded, ''Why?''

Jackie could not believe the extent of the woman's nosiness. ''I'd like to read about it, that's all.''

Willa walked over to the table where she kept the coffee urn. ''Have a cup?'' she asked. ''We can talk a spell.''

''No, thanks. I have to be going. I guess you don't have what I need.'' She turned toward the door, not about to be made to feel that she had to explain herself.

''Well, you're wasting your time chasing after Sam Colton. He's not interested in women.''

Jackie whirled about, heat rising to her face in embarrassment that she could think such a thing. ''I beg your pardon, but that's the farthest thing from my mind.''

Willa's lips curved in a knowing smile. ''Then what other reason would you have to learn about his business?

Seems to me you're just trying to bone up on what he does for a living so you can make yourself interesting to him, and—''

"And I resent your saying that," Jackie exploded. "Not that it's any of your business, but I happen to own half of that land up there now, and I want to learn all I can about what's being grown on it."

Willa gasped. "What are you talking about? The Coltons have owned that land as long as anybody can remember. I think you'd better see a lawyer—or one of them head doctors if you think you own any of Sam's farm."

Even though she was not about to explain how she came into the land, Jackie did not want to make an enemy of this woman if she could help it. Pleasantly she suggested, "Maybe you should ask Sam to explain it. I'm sure the two of you are old friends, and you don't know me at all." She held out her hand. "My name's Jackie Lundigan, by the way."

Almost grudgingly Willa shook it.

"Can you tell me where the nearest library is?"

"That would be up in Boone. They ought to have a good one, being it's a college town. It's not far—about fifteen miles or so."

Jackie thanked her and again started to leave, but Willa's apology held her back.

"Forgive me if I offended you, but what you said was such a shock. I still don't understand." She shook her head. "But it's none of my business. As for thinking you were chasing after Sam, well, you wouldn't't've been the first. There aren't many good catches up here in the mountains, I'm afraid, and he's one of the best."

"I'm sure he is," Jackie said for lack of knowing

what to say. She saw no reason to point out that looking for a good catch was not on her To-Do list.

"You need anything, you call me," Willa urged. "And don't be mad. I'm just a nosy old lady, but I'll make a good friend if you give me a chance."

Jackie drove the twisting, scenic road to the sleepy and picturesque little town of Boone, North Carolina.

She found the library by asking directions at the security guard's booth. A librarian showed her how to work their computer, and in no time at all she had printed out a treasure trove of information.

Afterward, she stopped at a Mom and Pop restaurant for fried country ham, red-eye gravy, stewed apples and the biggest biscuits she had ever seen. They were so good that she bought a half dozen to take home, along with a slab of cured ham.

Passing a roadside stand that was still open, she stopped and bought a jug of apple cider.

Life would be just about perfect, she thought as she crossed the mountain, if she could just work things out with Sam Colton. Maybe by reading up on the business they were in, he would see she was serious and meant to take an active part, not just collect her share of the money as Libby had done through the years.

And the money hadn't meant anything to Libby. She had turned it over to charity.

Jackie could also understand Libby's motive in passing the land along to her. She knew how badly she needed a new start in life and felt that a gift once bestowed out of deep and abiding love could only bring good things to whomever it was passed on to.

Jackie prayed she was right...and vowed to do everything she could to make it happen.

All she had to do was make Sam Colton see it that way.

Otherwise she feared she might have a war on her hands.

"Modern-day Hatfield and McCoys," she said aloud as she turned into her drive. "Only this time it will be Lundigan and the Coltons."

She wondered how many of them there were. If Sam didn't have a wife, he might have sisters or cousins who lived with him. If so, they would all be against her as they had been Libby.

Truly, she had her work cut out for her and decided she might as well get busy. As soon as she got the groceries put away, she would start studying. She wished she had thought to buy a lock for the front door. But she wouldn't have known how to install one, anyway.

She turned into the drive, then gasped and slammed on the brakes.

Sitting on the front porch, looking very tiny in one of the big oak rocking chairs, was her visitor of that morning.

She rolled down the window and waved. "Hi there, little bandit."

He did not wave back, just stared at her, his hands gripping the arms of the rocker.

Easing the car on into the yard, she gathered up her groceries and got out.

"You came back to see me," she said with a smile. "That must mean you aren't too scared of me. Are you going to tell me your name this time?"

He continued to stare, tight-lipped.

Undaunted, Jackie motioned him to come inside. "I have some pie left, and I remembered ice cream, too."

She had stopped on her way back from Boone and bought a half gallon of vanilla.

"And there's something else," she said, remembering the takeout she had bought at the restaurant in Boone. "Do you like fried ham and homemade biscuits?"

When he still didn't answer, she walked on in and busied herself getting out a skillet and then carving two slices of ham. When it was sizzling and the aroma was enough to make her own mouth water, she turned to go back to the porch to see if the boy was enticed enough to come on in.

She jumped, startled, to find him already seated at the table.

"My, you are a quiet one, aren't you? Well, welcome again." She poured him a glass of cold milk and went back to watch the ham so it wouldn't burn, talking to him all the while. "Maybe when you learn to trust me, you'll tell me your name and where you live. I'm happy for the company, believe me, but I don't think it's a good idea for a little boy to be wandering around up here. You could get lost. Anything could happen."

She scooped up the ham and put it between two biscuits on a plate and set it on the table. Before she could take a seat on the bench across from him, he was already eating.

She watched, amazed, as he wolfed down the food, then she asked—expecting him to refuse, "Pie and ice cream?"

He nodded.

"Now we're getting somewhere," she said brightly, leaping to her feet. "And before you know it that kitty cat that's got your tongue will let it go."

She ruffled his hair when she walked by him and was relieved to note he did not wince or pull away. Evidently he was just shy, and in time, everything would be all right.

She watched him devour the ice cream, then dared to suggest, "How about if you let me mend the knees of your jeans? I'm real good with a needle and thread."

For answer, he shoved back his plate, got down off the bench and quickly walked out the door.

Jackie stared after him and murmured, "Nothing like eating and running. Oh, well."

She cleared the table and stacked the dishes in the sink.

There would be time to think about the little bandit later and wonder who he was and where he lived. Now she had to think Christmas trees. Spreading her papers on the table she began to read.

Sam had just finished loading his truck with rolls of plastic for balling the roots of the live trees dug that day. It would soon be dark, and he needed to get back to the house and start supper. What to fix was the problem. He didn't mind cooking. He just got tired of making the same old things—fried hamburgers and pork chops. And he was sick of frozen dinners and fast food.

In the grocery store he went to the meat counter.

George, the butcher, came out of the back to greet him, wiping his hands on his apron. "Well, what's it going to be tonight, Sam? How about some nice stew beef? Just finished chopping some."

"Too much trouble. Takes too long." Sam pointed to the glass case and a tray of minute steaks. "Let me have a couple of those. They're quick and easy to fix. I hate to cook."

George reached into the case with a sheet of wax paper and picked up several slices and placed them on the scale to weigh. Then he wrapped them in brown paper, slapped on tape, scrawled the price on top and handed the package over with a teasing smile and said, "Maybe before long your new partner will start doing the cooking, and you won't have to."

Sam's hand, wrapped about the package, froze in midair. "What did you say?"

George laughed. "Oh, don't pretend with me, Sam. It's all over town about that flatland woman claiming she owns half your land. There's no need to be ashamed if you had to sell some off. Goodness knows, you've got so many acres up there you won't even be able to tell the difference."

Trying to hang on to his temper, Sam all but threw the steaks into his basket. "I don't want to talk about it," he mumbled, pushing the cart away so fast he bumped into Willa Kearney's cart.

"Sam Colton," she cried, "What's this about your selling off some of your land to that woman? Have you lost your mind? Your daddy is turning over in his grave."

"He's probably done that a lot, Willa," Sam said, righting his cart and giving it a shove. "And if you'll excuse me, I don't have time to talk right now."

"Well, come on in the Book Nook when you do," she called after him. "I want to hear all about this. She's a pretty girl, too. Seems real nice."

Real nice, he snorted, so mad that he wouldn't have been surprised if steam were coming out of his ears. The little twit couldn't wait to spread the word, obviously not caring how it was going to embarrass him when nobody had ever known anything about it. The least she could have done was give him a chance to let people know in his own way and his own good time.

She didn't understand anything about the way things were around here. How could she? She was a flatlander.

And would soon be one again if he had anything to do with it.

Chapter Six

Jackie awoke bright and early, truly determined that this day was the beginning of the rest of her life.

And that life, she vowed, was going to be the absolute best she could make it.

She was dressed in jeans, flannel shirt, down vest, and leather hiking boots—all ordered from a mail-order catalog.

Stepping out on the rear porch, she drank deeply of the pungency of the trees that closed off the back road to the cabin. She now knew what kind they were—blue spruce, with dark green to powdery blue needles. But they looked scrawny compared to the Fraser firs in the rows to the sides.

She had done her homework, reading till well after midnight. While there was, of course, still much to be learned from practical experience, she felt she knew enough to get started.

And getting started meant finding Sam Colton and telling him so, which was not something she was looking forward to.

It was cold, but with the knit cap on her head and the insulated gloves, she figured she would be fine outdoors. She had also ordered thermal socks, but they were on back order and not promised for several weeks. So she had on two pairs of regular socks, but her toes were still cold.

Wondering just how chilly it was, she looked at the thermometer on the porch, then shivered to see it was only thirty-seven degrees. "And it's still November," she mumbled with a shiver.

The temperature had really taken a plunge during the night. She had not needed a jacket the day before. Even little bandit, her mysterious visitor, had not worn a coat.

Thinking about him had interfered with her concentration the night before, because she could not get him off her mind. He had the saddest eyes of any child she had ever seen, and that bothered her. She wished there was something she could do to help, but if he wouldn't talk to her, then she was helpless.

She was relieved he did not look undernourished. Evidently he was just starved for really good food—like homemade apple pie and ham and biscuits. But she was going to have to find out who he was and where he lived, because his parents might not like a stranger feeding their child. Then, too, he might have special diet requirements she did not know about. What if he were a diabetic? she shuddered to think. No, she resolved then and there, until she knew something about him, she would not feed him again. And maybe telling him that would make him open up to her. It was certainly worth a try.

But, first things first. It was now time for a reckoning with her business partner.

She sat in her car at the end of the driveway leading up to the big white house, motor running, hesitant to drive on. Sam wouldn't be there. He would already have left to go to work. If she knocked on the door, she would have to answer questions about why she was looking for him.

Then, in the rearview mirror, she saw a truck approaching and hit the steering wheel with her fist and cried, "Yes!" and got out of the car to wave down the driver.

He slowed to a stop and poked his head out the window. "You got car trouble, ma'am? I can call a tow truck for you on my CB, but the Colton house is right up yonder, and they've got a phone."

"No. It's not my car," she quickly explained. "I'm wanting to find out where they're cutting trees today. I can hear the chain saws, but I have no idea where they're coming from because they're echoing all around."

He grinned. "No problem. I know where you can find the boss, 'cause I'm here to pick up a load." He hooked a thumb to indicate the empty flatbed behind him, stakes bundled and ready to be inserted to hold the trees in place.

"Then I can follow you. Thanks."

She returned to her car and waited for him to pass, then eased out behind him.

The road was deep with ruts, and several times Jackie feared she would get stuck again. The little car was not made for mountain driving, and it worried her to think how bad it was going to be in the snow and ice sure to come.

After ten minutes of bouncing and jouncing, she saw what looked like a big barn with several tin-roofed, open-fronted sheds lining the path to it. Fresh-cut trees seemed to be piled everywhere. Workers were busy at some kind of huge machine, but she could tell what it was doing.

Jackie looked around but did not see anyone resembling Sam.

She also realized she was the object of curiosity as workers began to slow in what they were doing to stare at her.

The driver looked in her direction, and she figured he told someone she was looking for Sam, because a few moments later he came out of the barn and started walking towards her.

She could tell by way he moved, shoulders squared, arms swinging, that he was annoyed. As he drew closer, there could be no doubt. His blue eyes were almost black with fury.

He waited till he was upon her before demanding, "What are you doing here? You're in the way."

Jackie yielded to sarcasm after she glanced around, respond with a shrug, "That's funny. I don't see me bumping into anybody."

"No, it isn't funny. Now I'll have to ask you to leave. We've got a lot of work to do around here, and I don't have time to waste on you."

She was struggling to keep cool, because he was really punching her buttons. "I should think time spent explaining operations to your new business partner could hardly be considered wasted, Sam. And I resent your rudeness, by the way. We have to try and get along."

"Get along." He snorted. "The only way we're going to do that is for you to just head back to your little cabin,

mind your own business and wait for your check. It'll be along after the first of the year, like always."

"Like…like always?" she sputtered, taking a step back in surprise. "You make it sound as if I'm used to getting money from you."

Sam took a quick glance around, saw everyone watching, and caught her elbow and gave her a tug. "Look. We can't keep standing out here like this arguing."

"You're the one who's arguing."

"And thanks to you, everybody is talking."

"About what?" She resisted as he tugged at her again. "And I'll thank you to take your hands off me. That's battery, you know."

He dropped her arm like it was a hot potato. "What do you mean? I didn't hit you."

"You don't have to hit. Battery is the unauthorized touching of a person's body without that person's consent. You didn't have my permission to touch me," she added almost petulantly.

Sam's hands went to his hips, and he stared down at her and shook his head incredulously. "What in the world are you talking about?"

Jackie felt herself coming unglued. Not only did she feel ridiculous for citing rules that nursing home employees had to learn by heart, but having him stand so close was becoming terribly unnerving. She could feel the heat of his anger, only it made her feel anything but frightened. Her eyes went to his shoulders, so broad, so strong, and his hand on her arm had been firm, yet, in a way, strangely caressing.

He had a little dimple beneath the corner of one side of his mouth, and when he had smiled so insolently, she had actually yearned to reach out and touch it with her fingertip. For a man so strong, so rugged, to have a dimple, well, it just made her feel like butter melting on a hot pancake.

Finally she replied, "Anyone working in a nursing home has to know the definition of assault and battery, otherwise we break laws or we can get sued."

He snickered. "And I'll just bet you know all the ropes where nursing homes are concerned, don't you?"

She did not like the mocking gleam in his eyes. "What's that supposed to mean?"

"Never mind. Well, are we going to stand here amusing everybody or will you go with me to my office where we can talk?"

Tossing aside the image of butter and pancakes, she crisply said, "Lead the way."

His office was a room in the corner of the barn. There was a desk, covered with papers, two chairs and a file cabinet.

She took one look around and blurted, "This is where you run our business?"

"Now listen—" He started to shake a finger but lowered it. He walked behind the desk and sat down, motioning her to also have a seat. "Look, I'm not in the habit of being rude, believe me, but if you'll pardon me for saying so, you'd try the patience of a saint—which I am far from being, I assure you."

He smiled.

There was the flash of a dimple again, and Jackie imagined she could actually smell butter and pancakes.

She squirmed in her chair. He was terribly attractive, in an almost feral sort of way. His presence also made her feel protected, somehow…as though if his arms were around her nothing or no one could ever hurt her, and—

Don't go there, her frantic brain commanded. She had

no business being attracted to him under the circumstances.

Under any circumstances.

It was her heart that spoke that time.

No men.

Not for a long, long time.

Independence.

Financial security.

Those things had to come first.

"Now look…" He spread his hands on the desk. "I was going to come to see you and talk about all this, but the season is here, and I've got trucks coming every day to pickup orders. It's a crazy time. But if you can just bear with me, we'll get everything settled once the rush is over."

She cocked her head to one side. "Settle what? I presume you talked to Mr. Burkhalter."

"I did. He confirmed what you said. He sent me some papers. They're up at the house in my other office. I haven't had a chance to look at them yet."

Jackie thought if his other office looked like this one he'd probably never see the papers again. "I repeat—what is it you want to settle?"

"You."

It was such a blunt answer that she recoiled. "Me? That's absurd. I'm the legal owner of that land, and I intend to take an active part in the farm. It's quite simple."

"No, it isn't. You might be the owner, all nice and legal, but morally you've no right to that land. Neither did Libby Pratt. Maybe if I try hard enough I can understand her hanging on to it, but not you.

"Now I know you probably went to a lot of trouble to get her to leave it to you," he continued, "but I don't want to talk about that, because it makes me sick to think of people preying on old ladies in nursing homes, and—''

Jackie bounded to her feet. ''Hey, you're way out of line, mister. I never preyed on her or anybody else. I had no idea she was leaving me that land, and I resent your accusation.

''In fact,'' she rushed on, face flaming as anger swirled, ''I demand an apology, or I swear I will pick up that phone right now and call Mr. Burkhalter and have him start a lawsuit against you that just might wind up with me owning this whole damn farm.'' She wasn't sure that was possible but was mad enough at the moment to threaten him with anything.

He also rose, clenching the edge of the desk as he leaned across it to put his face in front of hers and hotly declare, ''All right. I apologize. I have no proof. But everything points to it. Anybody would think the same thing.''

''Well, they would be wrong—just like you.'' She all but threw herself back in the chair. ''Now if you're through being absurd and ridiculous, let's get down to business.''

''Right.'' He likewise sat. ''How much?''

She blinked. ''How much what?''

''Money. To buy you out. Hell, I'll mortgage my half if that's what it takes to get rid of you. I'll call a friend of mine who's a Realtor, get him to do what's called an arm's length appraisal, and we'll go from there.''

''It's not for sale.''

He sneered. ''Of course it is. Everything is if the price is right. Name yours.''

''I don't have one. And I don't care how much you offer, I won't take it.''

Leaning back, he ran his fingers through his hair in agitation as he stared up at the ceiling and mumbled, "I don't believe any of this. What possible motive could you have in wanting to stay here and hang on to that land?"

"It's my home," she said quietly, matter-of-factly. "It's a new life. Something I desperately need... something Libby apparently also knew. That's why she left the land to me. And I intend to stay."

"It won't work."

"Of course it will."

"You're going to be snowed in soon. Do you have chains for that rust bucket you drive?"

"No, but I can buy some."

"Do you know how to put them on?"

"It can't be that hard to learn."

He chuckled, then asked, "What are you going to do when your well freezes up? No water. No plumbing."

Her sharp laughter wiped the insolent grin from his face. "What do I look like, Sam? A complete woosie? I'm going to trade my car for a four-wheel drive as soon as I can afford it. Meanwhile, I'm going to learn about things like frozen wells and water lines and make sure it doesn't happen.

"But, hey, we're getting off on the wrong track here," she said. "I didn't come here for you to tell me how rough things might get. And don't worry about me. I can take care of myself. All I need from you is to help me get started so I can be an active partner."

He groaned. "You'll only be in the way."

"No, I won't. Besides, from the looks of things, you can use some help in the paperwork department, anyway. I can do your bookkeeping for you."

"I have an accountant in town that does that."

"Well, I can help him. But first I want to go out in the fields and watch the harvest. What are you cutting today? Scotch pines? Balsams? Noble firs?" She was so proud of all she had learned the night before, albeit hastily, and even though she hadn't fully absorbed it and sorted it out.

She chattered on while Sam watched in silent amazement.

"So how many trees do you have planted per acre? It's usually two thousand an acre, and then only a thousand or fifteen hundred survive."

He continued to stare, saying nothing.

Jackie felt a twinge of unease. He did not look particularly impressed. In fact, he looked like he was trying to keep from laughing.

She had lost her confidence but felt the need to show her knowledge. "I know it takes a long time for a tree to be old enough to harvest—six to ten years."

"And fighting heavy rain, wind, hail and drought all the way," Sam said quietly. "It's not as easy as you make it seem."

"Well, I'll learn," she said lamely.

"Not from me. Get something straight." His eyes slitted. "I don't want you here. I can't make you leave, but I don't want you around. You'll get what's coming to you financially. Meanwhile, stay out of my way. That's the only way we're going to get along."

"Then we aren't going to get along," she snapped, worn out with his brashness. "And if that's your attitude, you can stay off my land."

"Stay off your..." He was so stunned, so infuriated, his voice trailed to a gasp of disgust, then, "You can't mean that. You'll lose the trees. You won't know what you're doing. And we'll both lose money. I can't fill my orders unless I harvest trees from Uncle Roy's land, too.''

"My land," she frostily corrected. "And I guess that's how it has to be, because I won't accept your terms."

Pressing his fingertips to his temples, Sam murmured, "I don't believe any of this."

"And another thing. What was that crack you made about people talking, thanks to me?"

"No one knew—till you told them—that Uncle Roy ever left that land to Libby. Everyone believed my family had always owned all of this land. Your letting them know otherwise is the biggest gossip they've had in these parts since the choir director's wife ran away with a satellite dish salesman three years ago."

Jackie wanted to laugh but didn't dare. "Well, it's not my fault. That's what you get for hiding the truth."

"It just never came up."

"You were all embarrassed, and you know it," she accused, then rushed on without giving him a chance to deny. "Furthermore, I think you—and probably your whole family—are too full of pride, anyway. None of you could accept the fact that one of your own loved someone so much he wanted to give her the only thing he had—precious Colton land.

"And another thing." Again she gave him no time for a comeback. "I still have a problem with that remark you made about me knowing the ropes about nursing homes...how you think I played up to Libby to get her to leave me in her will. Maybe you apologized, but you said everything points to it."

"That it does. Why else would she leave anything to a total stranger?"

"Be-because," she stuttered in her disgust and anger,

"sometimes people do things just because they're nice. It makes them feel good. But I guess you're so cynical you find that hard to understand."

"You have no right to call me cynical."

"Well, you have no right to insinuate that I play up to the elderly to get what I can out of them. I happen to like them. That's why I went to school to be a dietician so I could work at a nursing home and help make what time they've got left as pleasant as possible."

She threw up her hands. "Oh, why am I wasting my breath? You're going to think whatever you want to, and I've got other things to do—like find someone to run my half of the farm till I learn how on my own."

"You really intend to do that, don't you?"

"I don't bluff, Sam. And you're about to find that out."

She left, but he was right behind her, catching up to her in the main room of the barn. He caught her shoulder and spun her about. Then, seeing how she looked at his hand, dropped it and apologized, "Okay, okay. I'm battering you again. But I can't let you do this."

She blinked innocently. "Do what?"

"Hire somebody."

"I have the right."

"Of course you do, but it would only cause a lot of problems that neither you nor I want."

Something made Jackie hesitate. She had been about to go running out of the barn, leap into her car, race to town and begin asking around to find someone to work for her. Now, however, despite her annoyance, she wondered if maybe there was another reason Sam Colton was so arrogant.

She noticed, too, how unkempt he seemed. Oh, not dirty. Far from it. He smelled of aftershave, and his hair was shiny and clean. It was just that he seemed so thrown together, somehow. His shirt had seen better days. Like the little boy who had come to her cabin, his jeans could also use a mend here and there. And, glancing down, she saw that his socks didn't match. One was white and the other was blue.

She giggled.

He frowned. "Oh, you think it's funny that you want to turn my life upside-down."

She pointed to his socks.

"So?"

"I just think it's funny, that's all." She thought of Kevin and how meticulous he had been about his appearance. Everything had to be just so. He wore only the best designer labels, and it had irritated him that she accused him of being a walking billboard because he did not have the originality to select his own styles and colors. Instead he tried to impress people by wearing pricey clothes.

Sam retorted, "Lady, I'm a working man. I've got other things to do besides worry about matching up my socks in the morning, okay? Now let's talk about the problem at hand. I don't want you hiring somebody, so let's see what we can work out here."

"Well, I really don't want to hire anybody," she admitted. "So are you going to treat me like an equal?"

There was that twinkle in his eye again as he asked, "Is that what you want? To be treated as an equal in this business?"

Jackie could not pinpoint the reason but suddenly she felt uneasy. "Well, yes..."

"Then so it will be." He held out his hand. "If you can pull your share of the load around here, then I'll teach you all I can."

She looked at his outstretched hand. "No tricks?"

"Now why would I play any tricks?"

"Because you want to get rid of me. And you're still mad that people now know you don't own all the land up here."

He shrugged. "I'll admit I was annoyed at first. I don't like others knowing my business, but I guess they've got to have somebody—something—to talk about it, so to heck with it. As for wanting to get rid of you, that goes without saying, but I won't have to do a thing, because sooner or later you'll realize this is not the place for you. All I ask is a chance to buy you out when that happens."

"If it does," she assured, "I'll give you that chance, but until then, no funny business."

"No funny business."

She shook his hand.

He gripped it tightly. "One more thing."

She tried to pull her hand back, but he squeezed all the harder. "What? Let go..."

His grin was borderline wicked. "It's not battery. You gave me permission to touch you when you shook my hand."

"You're hurting me."

"No, I'm not. Now one more thing—"

"Anything, just let go."

"We're business partners. Nothing more."

She was confused. "I don't understand."

"Stay out of my private life. I don't even want you driving by my house. I'll have a backhoe in tomorrow to knock down those blue spruce blocking the road so you can get to the cabin that way."

"That...that is the silliest thing I've ever heard of," she sputtered. She gave her hand a hard yank, and he let go. "Why on earth would you chop down perfectly good trees just to keep me from driving by your house? I'm not going to bother you."

"Fine. But it's not altogether because I think you would. I just don't want to have anything to do with you beyond the business, which means I don't want to share a driveway. Besides, the spruces aren't so popular anymore."

Lifting her chin, she smugly added, "Because now most people have central heat in their houses, and a blue spruce will drop its needles in a warm room."

Seeing his surprise, she explained, "I've done my homework."

Grudgingly, he agreed that she had, but said, "There's lots more to growing Christmas trees than knowing the names of them."

She gave him a sweet smile. "Of course there is, and I'm looking forward to hearing you tell me all about it."

His sigh of resolve was so deep Jackie thought it had to have come all the way from the toes of his mismatched socks. "Okay then. Let's get started."

She walked with him to the machine she had seen earlier, wishing there was not such a feeling of hostility between them. And him saying he would clear the original road to the cabin to keep her from passing his house had been a jolt. But she had not made an issue of it, because something told her there had to be more to it than that. She just couldn't put her finger on what it was.

The machine, he explained, was a baler. Cut trees were rolled in on a conveyer. Then, very carefully, they were wrapped in plastic and laced with twine.

"It keeps them from getting banged around in shipping. Limbs aren't broken, and moisture inside the plastic keeps them fresh. But we can't do this to all trees, just those that aren't going so far. Otherwise, the moisture would cause mildew and rot.

"It they're going to a distant state, we pack them in larger bundles by just wrapping wire around them." He indicated a stack near the truck she had followed in. "Those are going to Florida."

"What are you going to do with the blue spruces you plan to cut down in my driveway?"

He shrugged. "I haven't thought about it."

"It's a shame to let them go to waste. Why don't we take them into town and give them to poor families who can't afford to buy a tree?"

"They aren't ready. They're too small."

"Not for small children," Jackie said with a grin.

He ignored her and led the way toward a shed and explained that was where live trees were processed. "I'll show you how the root balls are wrapped in burlap for planting after Christmas, and—"

Jackie came to a sudden halt, blinked in recognition, then cried, "It's him—my little bandit."

The boy froze where he stood, eyes going wide with recognition, then with fear. He turned and ran back the way he had come, disappearing between outbuildings.

"What did you call him?"

Jackie was puzzled because Sam sounded so mad. Looking at him, she saw that he very much was.

"I asked what you called him," he repeated, tone even colder.

"Little bandit," she said softly, hesitantly. "It...it wasn't meant to be unkind. You see, I found a fresh-baked pie missing from my windowsill, and I thought the raccoons had taken it. I had seen them on the porch the night before. Then I found out it was that boy, and I've been calling him little bandit ever since. He wouldn't tell me his name, and that's what people call raccoons. It was just a joke, that's all.''

Sam stared woodenly in the direction the boy had gone.

Hesitantly Jackie asked, "Do you know who he is?"

His gaze turned to her then, and she fought the impulse to wither beneath it.

"Yes, as a matter of fact, I do," he said in a voice so low she had to strain to hear. "He's my son."

Chapter Seven

Sam followed his son, and Jackie was right behind him.

"Where do you think you're going?" he asked testily.

"I want to meet him," she said.

"Another time. I need to talk to him." He quickened his pace and yelled, "Brian? Where are you?"

His tone was angry, and Jackie worriedly said, "You have no reason to be mad at him. He hasn't done anything."

"I don't want him bothering the neighbors."

She paused to throw her arms up in the air and cry, "What neighbors? I'm the only cabin around for miles, probably, and he sure doesn't bother me."

He had kept on walking, and she hurried to keep up.

"So don't say anything to him, please. I like having him come by. He's a sweet little boy. I know he's shy, because he never says anything, but I figure sooner or later he'll open up to me, and—"

He whirled on her then, and she came to a stop, rocking back on her heels.

"You think you know everything about everything, don't you? How people should eat, how to grow Christmas trees. Well, hear me loud and clear. You don't know a thing about my son, and you can stay out of anything that has to do with him. Got that?"

Hurt, humiliated, Jackie could only stare up at him as she blinked back tears.

He saw and was immediately contrite. "Look, I'm sorry. I know you meant well, and I apologize for biting your head off, okay? Just don't cry."

She heard desperation in his voice, could see pain etched in every line of his face.

Beyond him, she spotted Brian peering out from behind a stack of bundled trees that were ready for loading. There was something strange and sad about all of this. Sam had a son but not a wife. Jackie ached to ask questions but didn't dare. Not now, anyway.

"I'm so very, very sorry," she whispered, her heart going out to the little boy who continued to stare. "I had no idea he was your son…that he had no mother. But I'd still like to get to know him if you don't mind. I promise not to interfere."

"It's not that. I just don't want him bothering you."

"He's no bother, really."

"He has no business wandering around in the woods." He went over to Brian, with Jackie on his heels. "Son," he began, placing a hand on his shoulder, "I've told you before I don't want you going off by yourself."

Brian looked fearfully to Jackie.

"No, no, it's all right," Sam was quick to say. "She's not angry with you. And this is Miss Lundigan, by the way. She owns part of our farm now. It's a long story, and one day when you're old enough to understand, I'll tell you all about it. Meanwhile, I want you to stay away from her cabin, understand? If you don't, I'll have to punish you.''

At that, Jackie cried, ''No. Don't do that. I'm happy to have him visit me. Why, I'd even like to mend his little jeans if you don't care, and trim up his hair, and—''

''Jackie, please. I don't want you interfering, okay?''

He was trying to be calm, but she knew he was becoming more and more agitated.

''I only want to help.''

''And we don't need your help. We do fine by ourselves.''

Jackie knew she should let it go, then and there, back off and stay out of Sam's personal life, but the appealing way the boy was looking at her tore at her heart. He had enjoyed visiting her, she could tell…despite his silence. And now that she knew he had no mother, she felt drawn to him even more.

She brushed by Sam to drop to her knees before Brian. ''You don't do fine, do you?''

''He's not going to answer you.''

''And why not?''

''Because he's…he's got problems. Now leave him alone, please.'' To Brian he said, ''Go home. Hank is leaving with a load of trees. Go with him and he'll drop you off at the house. Stay there till I get home.''

Brian ran to obey.

Jackie stood and worriedly dared ask, ''What kind of problems?''

''Nothing that concerns you.''

The ice was back in his voice. Jackie knew if she

pressed on, he would only get mad, and this time might not apologize.

"All right. I'll butt out. But I want to emphasize that I don't mind him coming to see me. I enjoy having him around, and I love feeding him. What's wrong with that?"

He sighed. "What's wrong is that I have asked you— and now I'm telling you—to stay out of my personal life, Jackie. And you're going to have to do just that if we're to pretend to get along till you get enough of playing tree farmer and go back to the flatland where you belong."

She stared after him as he stalked away, shoulders set in that way he had when he was annoyed.

Yes, something was very wrong.

She was sure of it.

And when the time was right, she intended to find out exactly what it was.

But there was something else that had her in a quandary as well.

When he'd left, he'd brushed against her, and his touch had sent thrilling little tremors up and down her spine. It had been a long time since a man had made her feel that way...and maybe never with such intensity.

She was being drawn to him.

And something told her to pull away—fast.

Only she feared her heart was not listening.

Sam fought the impulse to look back.

He didn't care if those smoky green eyes of hers were brimming with tears again.

He couldn't let himself.

She was just another woman, like all the rest, out for money and nothing else. And as soon as she found out how rugged the life was, she'd hightail it quicker than a rabbit when it hears the dogs coming.

So he shouldn't care whether or not he spoke too brusquely and hurt her feelings.

But he did .

Because there was just something about her that inspired thoughts he shouldn't be having.

Which meant he was going to have to be really careful.

And also get rid of her as quickly as he could.

A week passed, then two. Jackie went every day to help do whatever she could to harvest the trees. The other workers were helpful but standoffish. Evidently word had spread that Sam was not at all happy with the situation, and they all wanted to stay out of it.

She seldom encountered Sam. The season was at its peak, and he was busy. He had told her that he would answer all her questions after Thanksgiving but till then, the priority was to harvest the trees and get them shipped.

She thought he had forgotten his vow to clear the spruces blocking the road to the back of her cabin—the road he wanted her to use. Then one morning she awoke to the roar of chain saws. Leaping out of bed and rushing to the window, she saw several men at work felling the sprightly little trees.

She bit her lower lip to think what a waste it was. No matter that they were shorter than the desired height of six to seven feet and needed to grow a few more years, they were still well shaped. They would make nice Christmas trees, especially for people who couldn't afford to buy one at all, much less the larger size.

Dressing quickly, she drove into town, having no idea

how to carry out her plan. Then she thought of Willa Kearney. Though she was nosy, there was no getting around that she was probably the one person in town who knew how to get something done.

Jackie was relieved to find the Book Nook open so early. It was not yet eight o'clock. As always, the delicious smell of coffee greeted her as soon as she opened the door, and she thought she detected the aroma of banana nut muffins in the oven.

"Hello? Anybody here?" she called, giving the door an extra shake to keep the bell over it ringing.

Willa appeared in the door at the back, wiping her hands. Recognizing Jackie, a grin took over her face. "Well, well. Fancy seeing you here. Especially so early in the morning. Did you find them books on trees you were looking for?"

"Yes, ma'am, I did," Jackie said. "I found everything I needed at the library in Boone. It's a nice town, too."

Willa wrinkled her nose. "Too crowded for me. Noisy, too, with all them college kids.

"By the way," she went on to say, "It was quite a shock for folks to find out about Roy Colton leaving his half of the farm to Libby Pratt. Sam told Hank, and Hank told everybody else. Nobody ever knew about it. The family kept it a secret. Guess they were ashamed of it."

Jackie couldn't resist suggesting, "Maybe they just don't like people knowing their business."

Willa thought about that, nodding as though it had never occurred to her, then said, "Well, it's a shame, that's what it is. Not that I've got anything against you, mind you, but Sam, poor soul, didn't need this. He's got enough troubles with that boy of his turning into a mute."

"I'm so sorry," Jackie murmured.

"Say, do you want some coffee?" Willa suddenly remembered to ask.

Jackie said she would love a cup. Willa seemed in a talkative mood, and she was eager to hear anything she might have to say about Sam.

Willa left her and returned a few moments later with two steaming mugs of coffee and a plate of hot muffins on a tray.

"Now then," Willa said, sinking into the faded, worn armchair next to the potbelly stove, "Come over here and sit down and tell me what's on your mind. I know you didn't come here for my cooking."

"Actually, I came to ask you how to give away some Christmas trees."

Willa's brows rose. "Won't that be a conflict with Sam?"

"I don't understand."

"Oh, he's got a little thing he does. I was surprised he went through with it last year after all the trouble with Donna, but I guess what you want to do won't make any difference."

Jackie was eager to know, "Who's Donna?"

"Sam's wife. Now about those trees, how many are there?"

"Probably a few dozen. I'm not sure. It was a test line of trees, so not many were replanted after the first harvest." She would much rather talk about Sam's wife but was afraid to ask questions. "Sam cut the ones that were planted across the old road to my cabin. Granted they're small, but I thought maybe there were some poor families who might like to have them, and you might know of a way we could do it."

"Well, if anybody can, I reckon I'm the one. I'll talk

to Preacher Lindon over at Little Creek Baptist—that's my church. Does Sam know about this?''

''He has no reason to. They were on my land. That makes them mine.'' Jackie helped herself to a muffin.

Willa said, ''I'll ask my Sunday school class if they want to take it on as a project.''

She leaned over and patted Jackie's knee. ''You're a sweet girl to want to do this. Now I'm glad Libby Pratt did leave you her land.

''So tell me,'' she settled back in the chair with her coffee, eyes shining with anticipation. ''Tell me everything you know about Libby. I knew her from the time we were children…knew how she loved Roy.'' She shook her head in sad remembrance. ''A real tragedy, him getting killed like he did, and for him to leave the land to her, well, it just shows how much he loved her.''

''That he did,'' Jackie agreed, thinking how if she told Willa what she wanted to know, it might lead her to confiding what happened to Sam's marriage. ''And Libby never stopped loving him, either.'' She then confided what she knew about Libby, her teaching career, her dreams of traveling, the accident and, finally, her untimely death.

''And I never knew about the land till her lawyer contacted me,'' Jackie was quick to emphasize. ''I was shocked she'd do such a thing.''

''Well, she had no family,'' Willa said. ''She never came back after her folks died. She must have thought a lot of you. And so do I,'' she hastened to add. ''Welcome to the mountains, dear. I hope you'll like it here.''

Jackie could stand the suspense no longer. She steered the conversation back to Sam. ''Well, I don't think Sam believes that I will. He's got me thinking I won't make it through the first winter.''

"Hogwash," Willa said. "Don't you pay any attention to anything that boy says. He's been through hell and back, and it's just been in the past few months that I've seen him pulling out of it. He's getting out a little, played some golf last month, I hear. And he goes fishing with my cousin, Bart, sometimes."

Willa drained the last of her coffee, saw that Jackie's cup was also empty, and got up for refills.

"It's just a shame about that boy," she said as she walked toward the counter and the coffeepot. "Sam's so crazy about him, but the fact is, he's retarded."

"Retarded?" Jackie echoed. "I don't think so. He seems bright to me. He's just shy, that's all."

"No. He's a mute. Can't speak a word. Not since his mother ran off with another man. Folks think the shock was too much for him, and he just lost his mind."

Jackie's head was reeling. Sam's wife had run away with another man? No wonder he seemed mad at the world. But to think it had caused his little boy to be mentally retarded was beyond comprehension.

"No," she said so forcefully that Willa stopped pouring coffee to stare at her.

"I don't believe that for one minute. He may be going through some sort of trauma because he misses his mother, but he'll get over it eventually. How long since his mother left?"

"A little over a year now, I think."

"Sam must have been really devastated," Jackie said, reminded of her own pain to discover Kevin had been unfaithful. Regardless of the fact that she now saw the marriage had been over for a long time, and love—if it ever truly existed—had gone, it was still humiliating, and it hurt.

Willa handed her a fresh mug of coffee, which she accepted eagerly.

"If the truth be known, I don't think Sam was all that surprised," Willa said. "There was talk they'd been having trouble for a long time. Donna never made a secret of the fact she hated it here. She was raised in Atlanta and used to big-city life."

"But there's peace and beauty and serenity," Jackie said, appalled that anyone could want more. "Besides, it's not that far to Asheville or even Charlotte. And Atlanta is right down the road."

"It wasn't enough for Donna, I don't guess."

"So why did Sam marry her in the first place?" Jackie asked, wondering why he hadn't realized how she was before proposing.

"Oh, it was a whirlwind thing. Sam was at a convention of tree growers in Atlanta. Donna was there at some kind of charity function. She was a member of Atlanta's high society, honey. And I know all this," she added with a proud smile, "because Joan told me."

"Who's Joan?" Jackie wanted to keep all the characters straight in the unfolding melodrama.

"She's Sam's mother. She lives in Charlotte now but has friends in Atlanta, and they told her all about Donna, how her picture was forever in the paper before she married Sam."

The plot was thickening, and Willa had Jackie's full attention. "So why did Sam's mother leave and go to Charlotte? Wasn't she from here, either? Did she hate it, too?"

"Joan?" Willa laughed. "Heavens, no. Joan loved it here. And she loved Sam's father to a fault. But when he died, she couldn't stand the memories and decided she needed to start a new life somewhere else, so she moved. She comes back now and then, though, and Sam goes and visits her when he can. He's crazy about her."

Jackie was glad to hear that. Kevin had treated his mother like dirt, and she'd always heard you could tell how a man would be with his wife by how he was with his mother. Not that she was thinking about Sam in those lines. It was just good to know her business partner had nice traits—at least that's the way she was determined to see it.

"Anyway," Willa went on, "everybody was shocked when Donna ran off with that man."

"And she hasn't been back to see Brian?"

"Not one time."

Jackie felt like crying. "Her own son. That's terrible. Does Sam know where she is?"

"I don't know. Linda—that's Sam's lawyer's secretary—said when he filed for divorce on the grounds of one year's separation, the only address he had was for her parents in Atlanta. Donna signed them and sent them back, but Linda said the postmark was California."

"I don't see how she could desert that little boy. Just walk away and never see him again. It's awful."

Willa agreed, "Yes, and it's worse because it's turned him into a mental case. There's nothing to do but send him away."

Jackie stared at her, aghast. "How can you say such a thing?"

"Well, it's not only me," Willa said defensively. "Everybody agrees. Especially Joan, and she's his grandmother so she should know."

Jackie asked, "How come she hasn't moved back here to take care of him?"

"She's got her own life now. She's remarried, to a very nice man. I met him when she came for Easter.

They travel a lot, and he's got plenty of money. She told Sam she's willing to pay for Brian to go to the very best institution money can buy. You see," Willa rushed to explain, "Joan thinks maybe Brian was a little mentally unbalanced all along and nobody noticed, and when Donna left, it just triggered it—turned him into a mute…made it obvious he's retarded."

Such an ignorant assumption annoyed Jackie greatly. But she knew it was a waste of time to try to convince Willa otherwise, so she abruptly changed the subject. "So when could you have someone pick up the trees?"

Willa thought a minute, then said, "Well, Christmas doesn't come long after Thanksgiving, you know, so we need to get busy. I'll make some phone calls tonight and see if I can't get the ball rolling to do it this weekend."

Jackie downed the rest of her coffee and left.

Was it already Thanksgiving? she wondered as she drove home. She had forgotten all about the holiday, because she had been so busy, and now remembering filled her with loneliness.

Impulsively she turned the car around and drove back to the grocery store. She bought a small turkey and fixings for all the trimmings, plus the makings for a pumpkin pie. Even if she were alone, she could have a nice Thanksgiving dinner, by golly, and, if she happened to see Sam, she would invite him and Brian to join her…though she doubted he would accept.

Still, she felt the need to be neighborly…and told herself that's all she was doing.

It was late afternoon when she set the pumpkin pie on the windowsill to cool. It was done to a turn, all golden brown on top with only a slight crack in the filling, and the crust had turned out perfectly—flaky and buttery.

As she leaned out the window, a movement in the shrubs caught her eye. She smiled as she cheerily called out, "Little bandit, is that you out there? If it is, you'd better not touch this pie till it cools, so come on in here and wait till it does, and I'll cut you a big slice and put whipped cream on top."

When there was no response, she went to the front porch and sat down in a rocker.

She didn't have long to wait. Brian poked his head around the corner of the cabin and stared at her uncertainly.

"It's all right," she said. "I know your daddy doesn't want you out in the woods by yourself, but I'll take you home and let you off far enough from the house so he won't see you, all right?"

Cautiously he walked toward the porch.

"But you have to mind your daddy," she said firmly as he came up the steps. "He worries about you and wants you to be safe, and so do I."

Brian sat down next to her, but she saw how he nervously gripped the rocker's arms.

Jackie chattered on, as though it was perfectly normal for her to talk and for him to listen without responding. She would ask him a question, then continue as though he had answered.

After a while, when the pumpkin pie had cooled enough, Jackie cut them each a big slice. Heaping on generous amounts of whipped topping, she added a few sprinkles of cinnamon along with toasted pecans.

Brian had followed her into the kitchen, and as soon as she put the pie before him, he ate, as always, like he was starved.

When he had finished, she glanced at the clock and winced. She had talked longer than she'd realized in her effort to draw him out of himself, and the afternoon had faded away. It would soon be dark.

She put his empty plate in the sink, then snatched up her car keys and motioned him to follow. "Come on, honey. I'm going to drive you home."

He sat right where he was and made no move to get up.

"Brian, you have to let me take you," she urged. "I can't let you go into those woods alone after dark. Your daddy doesn't even like you being out there in daylight."

Still, he didn't move.

Exasperated, she said, "Brian, if I let you walk home, your daddy will be so mad at me there's no telling what he might do. Why, he might even run me out of town on a rail."

She was teasing, but Brian bolted to his feet and quickly went outside to stand next to her car.

She was touched, because he obviously did not like the idea of her having to leave.

"Good boy," she murmured, and hurried after him.

She let him off at the mail box at the end of the driveway to his house and watched him in the twilight as he walked the rest of the way. After seeing a woman step out on the porch to meet him, Jackie turned the car around and started for home.

Suddenly a deer raced right in front of her car. She slammed on the brakes to keep from hitting him, and the car skidded sideways and into a ditch.

"Oh, no," she groaned, pounding on the steering wheel with both hands. It was history repeating itself.

In more ways than one, she realized with a shudder.

Sam's red pickup truck looked bright and big in her rearview mirror. Without bothering to speak to her, he went ahead and maneuvered to hook up the winch and pull her out.

Afterward, he walked up to her window and said without fanfare, "You've got a broken axle. I'll take you home and then call somebody to come out and tow it in Friday."

"Friday?" she cried. "But today is Wednesday."

"And tomorrow is Thanksgiving. I don't know how it was where you came from, Jackie, but around here folks take holidays seriously. Everything will be closed down. Now come on and get in."

The truck smelled like pines and firs and spruce trees. It was, she pleasantly realized, like being in a cloud of aftershave lotion. It was just that pungent and clean.

"I love it," she said, taking a deep breath.

Sam sent her a sideways glance. "What? The truck?"

"The smell of the trees. I love it."

"You'll get used to it," he said almost gruffly, "and then you'll gripe about it and say it smells like the stuff you clean toilets with."

She was quick to argue, "No, I won't, because it doesn't make me think about that."

"Then you'll gripe about how hard it is to get the resin out of your clothes and off your hands." His chuckle was cold, almost taunting. "Oh, yes, little lady, once you realize this isn't something out of a Currier & Ives Christmas card you'll be wanting to get out of here and be glad to accept my offer to buy you out."

Even now that she understood the reason he was so brusque, so cold, she was still annoyed by his obvious cynicism toward her. "I'm here to stay, Sam. And the sooner you realize that, the better we'll get along."

He was silent for a few moments as the truck bounced along on the road toward her cabin. Then, remembering, he asked, "What are you doing over on this side, anyway? My boys cleared that back path out for you. They even smoothed it over. They also told me you wouldn't let them haul the trees off."

She pressed back against the seat, as though going into a kind of battle mode. "I told you I don't want those trees to go to waste. Besides, do I have to remind you they were on my land? They belong to me."

"And what, may I ask, are you going to do with them?"

"I talked to Willa at the Book Nook. She's going to have her Sunday school make it their project to see that they get to needy families."

"Fine," he said coldly.

She turned to glare at him. "Do you have a problem with that?" She was surprised to see a mysterious smile spread slowly across his face.

"No," he said softly. "I don't begrudge it at all."

And then the smile faded and was replaced by his mouth becoming a thin, hard line as he asked, "Now will you tell me what you were doing over here? It's closer for you to get to town by your back road."

She folded her arms across her chest and stared doggedly ahead. She was not about to tell on Brian.

But as it turned out, she didn't have to.

"You brought Brian home, didn't you?"

Her face, along with her quick intake of breath, gave her away. "You won't punish him, will you? I'm sure he was just out for a walk and happened by my place and smelled the pumpkin pie I'd just made. We got to talking, and—"

"Talking?" he all but shouted. "What do you mean?"

"I was talking, and he was listening. The time just slipped away. I didn't want him out walking after dark, so I brought him home."

"I won't punish him, but I will have another talk with him.... And you, too," he added sharply.

He had driven right up to her porch. He did not turn off the engine, instead reaching across the seat to open her door for her.

She got out but paused to ask, "What about?"

"Your meddling in my business," he snapped. "But it will have to wait till after Thanksgiving. I'm taking Brian to visit my mother."

He shut the door.

The window was rolled halfway down, and she called through it, "Fine, I'll be looking forward to it."

He drove away, and she stared after him until the red glow of the taillights disappeared.

Then she touched her breasts.

His arm had brushed against them as he had reached to open the door. It had sent a warm rush through her body, and even now she imagined she felt the heat.

Dangerous reactions.

Dangerous thoughts.

And if she didn't get a rein on them...and on her heart...then she might be headed for big trouble.

Sam Colton was obviously carrying a lot of baggage where women were concerned, so he was not a man she had any business getting involved with. But more and more, lately she found herself thinking about him and, yes, much as she hated to admit it, she was very much attracted to him. It was a one-way street to heartache.

And she had to back off, think of him only as a business partner and nothing more.

The only thing was, her heart did not seem to be listening.

Chapter Eight

Jackie admitted to being a bit lonely during Thanksgiving. Though the weather was nice—crisp and cold with brilliant blue skies and a gleaming sun, she found herself missing being around holiday festivities. If not for her car being out of commission, she knew she would have sought out a nursing home to visit residents who would otherwise have no company.

What she needed, she had decided, was a telephone to keep in contact with the outside world. But the cabin had never been wired, and lines had not been run from town. When she applied, she was told there was a long wait list for rural areas.

She busied herself around the cabin, making curtains for the windows and painting the cupboards in the kitchen.

At first she felt very self-sufficient and was proud of herself for her accomplishments. But then she discovered a leak under the kitchen sink and had no idea how to fix it. Kevin had always called repairmen for the least little thing, and she'd never been handy with tools.

Then she discovered she hadn't ordered enough firewood and spent a night shivering under every blanket she could find to pile on the bed. The next morning she tried to chop some from the woodpile, but the ax was so dull it would have been hard put to cut butter.

Her confidence began to wane, and she spent the rest of the day going over her budget to see if she could afford to buy more wood, as well as hire a plumber to fix the leak. But it was no use. She was running out of money, because she had spent more than she'd planned on fixing up the place.

Mr. Burkhalter had told her there might be a delay in her receiving the year's farm income that would have gone to Libby due to all the probate.

She'd had only one conversation with Sam over finances, and that had been when she'd bluntly told him that after this harvest she intended to run her hundred acres on her own. He'd laughed, told her again she would not make it through her first winter, then pointed out that he could not go along with her getting all the profits from trees that he had planted and nurtured on her land that would be ready to cut the next year. So they agreed to share the future season fifty-fifty, which meant she would only get half the money she would have received otherwise.

Things looked grim, but she was determined to remain undaunted. If she had to take a part-time job somewhere, so be it. She was dreading the talk Sam wanted to have, and every day she expected him to come driving up to her door.

He came on Sunday, towards evening.

She was sitting on the porch, enjoying the lovely weather and keeping a wary eye on dark clouds gathering to the west. The TV was on the blink, but she had a radio and had heard there was the chance of snow showers in the mountains. The temperature was steadily dropping, and she wished she'd found a way to get some wood, because she was almost out. Nights had been cold, and she wasn't used to the harsh temperatures and had used the stove probably more than she should have.

She watched as Sam drove slowly up the road, careful not to scatter gravel. That was a good sign. That meant he was calm, not upset and ready for battle. But what was there to fight about, anyway? If he wanted her to stay out of his business, fine. She would try to do just that, though it was going to be next to impossible to turn Brian away if he came around. As for anything else, like her accepting his offer to be bought out, forget it. North Carolinians were called Tar Heels because of how state soldiers had dug in their heels to fight in the Revolutionary War, and she was going to do the same thing— dig in and fight.

He parked the truck, got out and quietly closed the door. He was wearing a brown cap emblazoned with the National Rifle Association logo, a red flannel shirt and khaki pants that looked like they just came out of the dryer.

He was smiling.

A good sign.

She smiled back. "A belated 'Happy Thanksgiving.' How was it?"

He settled in the rocker next to her. "Okay, I guess, but I'd rather have been home. I don't like big cities, but my mother insisted on having an early Christmas for Brian. She's leaving for Europe, and when she comes back she'll be going to Florida till spring. Her husband has a condo in Sarasota.''

''I've always wanted to go to Europe,'' Jackie said wistfully. ''But never had the means. London, Paris, Rome. I'd love to do them all.'' She waved her arm in gesture.

Sam lips curled in a sneer. ''Typical woman. A gadabout. Always wanting to go somewhere.''

She suspected that her enthusiasm for traveling had ignited memories of his ex-wife, but she was not about to be lumped into the category of flighty women. ''No, that's not true. Most women like the comfort and security of a home and a routine, but it's normal to want a change once in a while. So just because I say I'd like to visit Europe, or anywhere else for that matter, does not make me a gadabout.''

He gave her a strange look. ''Well, pardon me. I didn't mean to ruffle your feathers.''

She let it drop. She had made her point. ''So how is Brian? Did he enjoy visiting his grandmother?''

''He seemed to.'' He turned in his chair so he could look her straight in the eye. ''Now that you've brought him up, let's get to the point of why I'm here, Jackie.

She braced herself. ''Go ahead.''

''I think you're crazy to want to stay here, but I can't stop you. What I can do, however, is ask you one more time to stay out of my business.''

''Which means you want me to turn your child away. Sorry. I can't do it. I agree he shouldn't be out in the woods by himself, but he seems to know his way. But to run him off? No way.''

''Very well,'' he said with a nod of concession. ''Then I'll just have to try harder to make him stay home. I've been thinking of hiring a housekeeper.

Maybe it's time that I did. That will solve one problem, at least.''

"You have more?" she asked, not liking the way he was looking at her like everything was her fault.

"As a matter of fact I do. I wish we could have worked something out as to what you were going to tell people. It's kind of embarrassing for people to find out someone besides a Colton has owned it all these years.''

Jackie could not help bristling over that. "Well, you want to know something, Sam? I don't care. You and your family shouldn't have been so prideful. What Roy Colton did was nothing for you or any of your relatives to be ashamed of. It was a sweet gesture of love, and if you ask me, the world could use a little more of that. And what's more, I'm certainly not ashamed of how I came to own it, so don't expect me to act like I am.''

"I like to keep my business to myself," he returned.

"Well, it wasn't your business. It was Libby's. Now it's mine.''

He was silent for a moment, absorbing that, then grudgingly suggested, "Well, it might be good if you learned not to talk so much when you're in town. Especially around Willa. She's got a heart of gold, but she's a big gossip.''

"That she is." Jackie leaned back and folded her arms across her bosom. "She told me all about your wife leaving you and how Brian hasn't spoken since she did.''

"I might have known," he said with a curse under his breath.

"Want to talk about it?"

Her impertinence caught him off guard, and he laughed. "Are you serious?"

"Of course I am. It helps to talk about your problems."

"I don't have any...not anymore."

"Then what about Brian? If his mother abandoning him caused him to lose his ability to speak, I'd say that's a real big problem. What are you going to do about it?"

"That's my business," he practically shouted.

She began to rock to and fro. "You don't have to get so huffy. I'm only trying to help."

"I don't want him forming any kind of bond with you, Jackie."

"And why not?" she challenged, fighting anger as she knew he was also doing. His mouth was firmly set, and there was an angry tremor in his voice. "I should think you'd be glad for him to want to be with a woman after how his mother deserted him."

"That's just it. He might be looking to you for the love he craves from his mother, and when you leave, he'll go through another upset, and I don't want that."

"And how many times do I have to tell you I'm not leaving?" she cried. "I like it here. It's taking some getting used to, but I'm a survivor. I've been through a lot."

"You?" he snickered. "You're a cream puff. All you've ever done is plan menus for old people. You've probably never had a stressful moment in your life."

She stared at him long and hard, trying to decide whether to let him into her private side, the hidden part that still humiliated her to think about. Finally she knew she could not let him get away with thinking she'd had a life of ease.

Drawing a deep breath, she let him have it. "For your information, Sam Colton, I've been through more stress than I ever dreamed possible. My husband dumped me after I worked day and night to put him through medical school, then got a quickie divorce in Mexico so he could marry the daughter of the surgeon whose very lucrative practice he's joining.'' Her smile was tart. ''He also had to hurry up, because she was four months pregnant.

''All of that,'' she said after pausing to catch her breath, ''led me here. Libby leaving me this land, this cabin, was a godsend, because I needed a 180-degree change in my life to help me get over being kicked in the teeth. So don't think I won't survive here, because I assure you I will.''

''That's quite a story,'' he said quietly, politely. ''And I'm sorry. I didn't know.''

''Neither did I,'' she said flippantly, ''till he started sleeping on the sofa and staying out all night when he wasn't working at the hospital. Something told me it wasn't my snoring.''

''You snore, do you?''

Their eyes met, held, and they burst into laughter.

''It's not funny,'' she said.

''I know,'' he said gently. ''I was just trying to cheer you up. I guess I was out of line.''

''Nobody trying to cheer somebody up is ever out of line in my opinion.'' She patted his shoulder in a gesture meant to lighten the moment but immediately drew back her hand. Touching him had ignited a funny feeling in the pit of her stomach, and she was afraid he might notice.

''I suppose not,'' he said. ''Besides, nobody knows better than me how it feels when someone betrays you. It can really knock you for a loop.''

''But life goes on, Sam. Things change. People change. Eventually wounds heal. Sometimes there are scars. But we have to forget about them or we can't go on. I certainly don't intend to be so bitter over Kevin that all I do is brood about what happened.''

He surprised her by asking, "Do you think that's what I'm doing?"

"In a way, yes," she said with candor. "I think it's why you resent me, to tell the truth. You're bitter toward all women, and that's not a good thing."

He snorted. "Women don't mean anything to me. I don't intend to ever get tangled up with one again. It's my son I'm concerned about—angry about—because of what Donna did to him when she left."

"And did that come as a shock?" she gently prodded. Now that he was opening up to her, she wanted him to keep talking. It was the only way they would ever become friends. That was important since they were partners...and she told herself that was all she cared about.

"Not altogether. The same way you said it was with you, we hadn't been getting along in quite a while. Still, I didn't have a clue what she was planning, and..." His voice trailed off.

Jackie watched as he stared into the distance, as though he could see into the past, wincing as he did so, for the vision was obviously painful.

Abruptly he said, "Look. I didn't come here to get off on this. And we shouldn't have discussed your personal life, either. I just wanted to have it understood that we keep things between us strictly business. And that includes your discouraging Brian to come here, all right?"

She gave her head a firm shake. "Sorry. I've already told you—I won't run him off."

He gave a weary sigh. "Okay, then. I'll handle it." He got to his feet.

Jackie also rose, walking with him to the edge of the porch. "So where will work be going on tomorrow?"

"At the main sheds. We've got some last-minute bundling to do. With only four weeks to Christmas, we're about finished."

"Then what?"

"We clean up. I pay the help, then get all the paperwork together to send to my accountant for year's end. After that, I'll be planting seedlings."

"Your accountant..." Jackie said slowly, hesitantly, not wanting him to know how desperate she was becoming for money. "When did he usually send Libby's check, do you know? I'm just curious."

Sam said he had no idea. "I never worried about it. Maybe you should call your lawyer and ask him."

"I will next time I'm in town. Meanwhile, could you make some phone calls for me?" She hated to ask but had no choice. "I need to check on my car. I don't know if they've even towed it in or not."

"If they didn't, it's been stolen," he said, grining. "Because it's not there anymore."

She clapped her hands in mock delight. "That would be a blessing, only I doubt anyone would want the old klunker."

"Sure, I'll check on it."

"And if you could order me some firewood, I'd appreciate that, too. I'm sorry to have to put you to so much trouble, but I can't get the phone company to put my phone in. They say there's a wait list for phone lines on these back roads, and nobody has ever asked for them to be run this far back."

"That's right. Nobody ever lived here for any amount of time." He seemed unable to resist pointing out, "That's another reason you'll be ready to move before winter's over, Jackie. I can't imagine you staying here without a phone.''

''I'll manage,'' she said, jutting her chin up ever so slightly. It would take more than not having a telephone to run her off.

''Anything else?''

''The name of a good plumber. The kitchen faucet leaks.''

She could tell he was trying very hard not to smile.

''Well, you'd better get used to roughing it, because this is only the beginning.'' He rolled down his sleeves as he looked up at the sky. ''We might be in for some bad weather.''

''The radio says snow.''

He pursed his lips, then shook his head. ''I don't think so. It doesn't smell like snow.''

''Smell?'' she asked in wonder.

''That's right…smell. If you stayed here long enough you'd get to know it, too.'' He went down the steps and walked to his car.

Jackie called, ''Well, if it does, and I don't show up for work tomorrow, come look for me in a snowdrift.''

Soberly, he pointed out, ''If it snows, we don't work, Jackie.''

He was treating her like a child, and she resented it to the point of grinding her teeth together but was not about to let him know it. ''Then I'll see you tomorrow, Sam, with bells on.''

She went inside and watched through the window as he drove away. *She* might be looking forward to the next day, but it was obvious Sam was not…just as it was quite apparent that nothing would make him happier than for her to pack up and move out.

But it wasn't going to happen, she promised herself,

anymore than she was going to allow her heart to keep tripping out every time he was around.

Sam Colton, due to all the bitterness embedded in his soul, was a one-way ticket to heartache.

And Jackie had had enough of that to last a lifetime.

In his rearview mirror, Sam watched the mellow glow coming from the cabin windows until he turned onto the main road.

The woman was trouble with a capital T.

Maybe she was cute and perky and pleasant to be around. She was still meddlesome, opinionated and, worst of all, a flatlander.

But, most importantly—and the biggest thorn in his side—she was sitting on land that was not rightfully hers.

He supposed he should have known it would happen sooner or later, that Libby Pratt would die and pass title to somebody else. But he had assumed the new owner would be content, as Libby had been, to collect his or her share of the profits every year and stay away. After all, unless someone was an avid skier, this part of North Carolina was not a place anyone wanted to be in the dead of winter—as Jackie Lundigan was soon going to find out.

Already she was running out of firewood. That meant she was not taking the chilly weather very well and keeping the wood stove going full blast.

She obviously had money problems or she'd have traded her car for a four-wheel-drive vehicle, which was a must.

She was in for rude awakenings in many ways, and he almost felt sorry for her.

But not quite.

After Donna, Sam had no patience with any woman who ventured out of her element…away from all that she was used to. Sure, they had the right to try something different, to make a new life—but not when it wrecked somebody else's.

Like his.

Like Brian's.

Sitting on that porch had brought the memory back, and, along with it, the pain that he never failed to experience with he looked at his speechless son.

Donna had asked him for time and space to decide whether to agree to his proposition that they go to a marriage counselor. So he had moved into the cabin. It had required cleaning and some fixing up, but he hadn't minded. It kept him from thinking too much about the misery of his marriage.

His mother had told him he should have known better than to marry a girl who had grown up in the city. The isolation had been hard enough on her, she'd said, and she was born and bred in the mountains. But things had happened fast. Sam had taken one look at Donna and fallen helplessly, hopelessly, in love…or so he thought. Now, looking back, he knew it had only been an illusion, because he was young and eager to fall in love and have a family.

Sam turned into his driveway and saw that Hank Cooley's truck was in the yard. He had come to pick up his wife, Bonnie, who had agreed to stay with Brian while he went to have his visit with Jackie.

He slowed. Hank was early. It wasn't quite five-thirty, hardly dark yet, and he'd told Bonnie he'd probably be gone till six. So now he wanted a few minutes to get himself together in case his stress was showing. There had been enough talk lately, what with Jackie spilling the beans about Libby. But he couldn't really fault her for that. After all, she was right when he said his family had been prideful. Still, it wasn't anybody's business, so there was no reason to broadcast it.

So his mind went racing back to what he had felt as he sat in the rocker, how it was like watching a video of that day that seemed forever burned into his memory.

He shuddered there in the cocoon of the truck's cab, the dash lights a mellow glow as though guiding him back through that hurtful, humiliating time.

He knew why he had tried to keep the marriage together, and it wasn't because he loved her. Like water one drop at a time eroding a stone, she had worn away whatever feelings he'd had for her with her vicious tongue, her coldness in bed and, yes, her physical abuse—a cup of coffee thrown in his face, a book slammed against the back of his head. Once she had even attacked him with her nails.

But never once had he hit her or tried to defend himself. He just got away from her as fast as he could, and the wounds on his heart deepened and became scars that did not fade.

His mind took him back once again to that fateful day. It was early morning, and he had been slow getting up after staying up most of the night going over bills. Tree cutting had just begun, so it was to have been several months before he would have much money, and Donna had maxed out all of her credit cards. She was buying clothes right and left, makeup, perfume, lingerie. When he told her she had to slow down, she had petulantly said she was trying to look nice for him, so why was he fussing when he was always after her to try harder to make the marriage work?

Dreading confrontation but knowing it had to come,

he had poured a second cup of coffee and sat down in the rocker to think about what he was going to say to her…how he was going to break the news that she left him no choice but to cancel all her credit cards, at least until he could catch up on the payments.

At first he had not believed his eyes, thinking it had to be a play of light from the early sun dappling down through the Fraser firs at the edge of the forest. Or perhaps it was a fawn, left by its mother for a morning nap while she went in search of breakfast.

Then he bolted to his feet.

It was not a play of light.

Neither was it a fawn.

It was Brian.

He had leaped off the porch and raced across the yard.

Brian was curled up in a fetal position and appeared to be sleeping. He was still in his pajamas, which were wet with dew.

He had gathered him up and taken him inside, quickly wrapping him in a blanket. He lay with his eyes open, staring blankly, but said not a word when Sam asked him over and over what he was doing there…how he got there.

He did not seem to be hurt, so Sam had put him in the front seat of the truck and driven like a bat out of hell for home to find out what was going on. All kinds of horrible thoughts ran through his head. Donna had to be hurt, and Brian had found her when he woke up and then made his way through the path in the woods to the cabin to find him and tell him. Only he wasn't saying anything and appeared to be in shock.

When he reached the house, Sam had left him in the truck and raced inside, calling Donna's name over and over as he hurried toward the bedroom.

And that was when he found the note propped on the pillow:

> Dear Sam,
> There is no easy way to say I am leaving you. My life is with someone I realize I have loved since my college days
> Brian will be happier with you. After all, he is a Colton—something I can never become and do not want to be.
>
>   Donna

He had sat on the side of the bed and read the lines over and over till his eyes were burning, his vision blurred. Then finally he remembered Brian and ran back to the truck to bring him inside.

He had dressed him in dry clothes, then rocked him to sleep, and only when he was quiet did he phone Donna's mother in Atlanta.

She had apologized for what her daughter had done and said she had cried when Donna called her from the airport and told her about it. Donna had been on her way to a holiday in the Caribbean with her lover and said the only thing that bothered her was how Brian happened to wake up as she was leaving and seemed very upset. But she was sure he'd get over and that Sam would, too, and everyone would see it was for the best.

Sam had slammed the phone down in the cradle so hard it had broken.

And in that anguished moment, as he thought of his son crying for his mother not to leave him, he knew it was good she was not there, for he'd have lost all control, for sure.

And to have left him, knowing he would be alone till morning was unconscionable.

It was just a miracle he was all right...a miracle he'd not gotten lost in the woods but evidently had waited till first light before starting out to try and find his daddy.

When several days passed, and Brian refused to speak, Sam had taken him to a doctor who was at a loss as to the reason. He said in time he might get over it. But now, over a year later, it did not look as though he were going to.

Sam started the truck moving again.

He did not want to send his son away, did not want to be without him for even a day. But it was constant agony to know he was still suffering from the anguish of losing his mother. She'd not returned, and there had not been a letter or a phone call. Neither had he heard from her family.

So he felt as if he bore the weight of the world on his shoulders, trying to keep the farm going and take care of his son, and he did not need a flatlander moving in and complicating things.

Especially a female flatlander who had a way of igniting feelings and emotions he had sworn never to feel for any woman, ever again.

But, he decided with a weary sigh, it appeared she was going to stay, for a while, anyway, and he supposed he would have to make the best of it.

Only he intended to keep it on a business level.

And he wanted Brian to stay away from her.

He would not, by God, see him hurt again by losing someone he cared about.

And Sam vowed, then and there, to keep a check on his emotions, as well.

He would just have to stop thinking about how it

The Silhouette Reader Service™ — Here's how it works:

Accepting your 2 free books and gift places you under no obligation to buy anything. You may keep the books and gift and return the shipping statement marked "cancel." If you do not cancel, about a month later we'll send you 6 additional novels and bill you just $3.57 each in the U.S., or $3.96 each in Canada, plus 25¢ delivery per book and applicable taxes if any.* That's the complete price and — compared to the cover price of $4.25 in the U.S. and $4.75 in Canada — it's quite a bargain! You may cancel at any time, but if you choose to continue, every month we'll send you 6 more books, which you may either purchase at the discount price or return to us and cancel your subscription.

*Terms and prices subject to change without notice. Sales tax applicable in N.Y. Canadian residents will be charged applicable provincial taxes and GST.

made him feel all warm inside when Jackie smiled at him, or how her bright, friendly eyes were as green as new spring grass.

He also swore to stop thinking how good it would feel to touch her, hold her, and—

He gave his head a vicious shake.

It would be hard, but she would not be around much longer.

At least he hoped that was how it would be, because he did not like to think of the consequences if she stayed.

Chapter Nine

Sam cursed himself for the rush that went through him to hear Jackie call his name.

"Hi, Sam. Sorry I'm late, but I forgot I was going to have to hike through the woods to get here. Did you think to call and ask about my car?"

To hide his pleasure over seeing her, he was brusque. "No, I haven't. I've got a farm here to run, Jackie. I don't have the luxury of sitting back waiting for someone to mail me a nice, fat check every year."

She stopped a few steps from where he was feeding rope into the bundling machine. "I think you're being unfair. I've tried to pull my share of the load around here, and you know it. And it hasn't been easy, either, with you being so huffy about showing me what to do."

He scowled. "What can you do besides get in the way and ask me to be your personal secretary? It's not my fault you don't have a phone. I didn't invite you to live where you can't have one. And don't blame me because you didn't have sense enough to know you needed a four-wheel-drive up here.''

She was cold, because the wind had picked up and felt as though it was cutting right through her down jacket. There was also no sunshine, because the sky was thick with gray-black clouds. She had heard on the radio that snow was forecast. She'd had second thoughts about taking off through the woods but was determined to do her part. And this was what she was going to have to work with?

Rubbing her gloved hands together, she said, ''You know, for a little while there last night, I almost started thinking you were human...that we could get along. But I guess you've got a crappy attitude that you just can't keep down for very long. So maybe I'll just turn around and go home and have some hot vegetable soup I've got simmering on the stove and let you stand out here in your misery and freeze.''

She turned on her heel.

He yelled at her, ''Get back here. You want to be a part of things? Well, that includes putting up with my attitude when I've got one. So here—'' He threw a bundle of rope at her, which she barely managed to catch. ''You've watched the men do this...watched me do it. So get busy. I've got to start loading the last of the trees.''

It was times like this Jackie wondered how she could be even remotely attracted to someone who could be so cranky. But she had only to see the shadows in his blue eyes, and the sad twitch at the corners of his lips, to know it was not the real him. This was a man haunted by the worst kind of betrayal, as well as tormented by his son's affliction. So the way to react, she decided, was to ignore him and concentrate on what needed to be done.

She busied herself threading the bundler. She had seen it done enough times to know how. And in no time at all, the fragrant trees were gently rolling in place and being secured for their trip to market.

Sam worked nearby doing a much harder job. A late order had come in for a load of trees that could be planted after Christmas. That meant the root ball had to be bundled in burlap and secured with ropes. The trees were heavy, and he had to use a forklift to get them on the flatbed truck.

They worked in silence for a time, and then Jackie finally had to ask, "Would you mind telling me where everyone else is today? Seems funny to me there's just the two of us."

"Hank is down with his back, but he said he'd be here tomorrow. I've let the seasonal help go. There wasn't much left to do that me and Hank can't handle."

"Only it's not you and Hank," she could not resist sarcasm. "It's you and me."

"Griping about a little hard work? Well, get used to it, sweetheart. It's called the farming life."

"I can handle it. And don't call me sweetheart." She changed the subject. "Where is Brian?"

"With Hank's wife. She's been away, visiting her mother in Asheville. I thought he'd be okay by himself the few times I left him at the house, but that's when he was sneaking off, and I didn't know it. It won't happen again."

"He seems like such a nice little boy," Jackie said with a wave of pity. "It's so sad he's so troubled."

"He's going to be fine," Sam said, almost angrily. "He just needs time."

Jackie decided not to continue to broach such a touchy subject, instead gesturing to the trees she had just bundled. "These are really nice. Are there many of this kind on my land?"

She noticed he did not wince as he usually did when she made reference to her land.

"Yes, as a matter of fact there are more Frasers over there than anything else. They grow real well up here, but I'm also trying to get a good crop of balsam, Douglas and white pines going. It's more profitable to have a variety. But the Fraser is definitely the most popular. It's been chosen for the official White House Christmas tree eight times, more than any other variety."

He pointed to the one he was working on. "It takes a while to get them this big, though. Twelve years to grow six to seven feet. For other varieties it might take as long as fifteen. But the average is seven."

She had finished her work and walked over to lean against the truck to watch as he finished his. "You said something about starting seedlings soon."

"Yeah. I'll do that from seed in my nursery, then transplant them in about two years to field beds."

"And I suppose you've got some ready to be planted where you cut this year's harvest."

He nodded, took a deep breath, and gave the rope he was pulling around the burlap one last, hard tug. Then he explained, "I've got about two thousand to set per acre, and I harvested about a hundred acres this year."

Jackie gave a low whistle. "That's a lot of digging."

The wind was really starting to howl, and she was fighting to keep from shivering so he wouldn't see and make a snide remark.

Finally, however, he did notice, and he pointed to his truck and told her to get in. "I'm almost finished here. I'll drive you home."

She glanced worriedly at the sky. "Do you smell snow yet?"

"Nope," he said with confidence. "Nothing to worry about. There's still time for you to get down to the flatland before real winter sets in."

"I have no intentions of doing that."

"Why stay? You've got no reason to."

"Excuse me?" His back was toward her, and she could not see his face to know if he was teasing. Something told her he wasn't.

He continued working, did not turn around. "I asked why you're staying. There's nothing else to be done till spring."

"You said you were going to plant seedlings."

"That's no big deal."

"It is to me when I've never done it before. So leaving is out of the question. Besides, this is my home now."

He straightened, shoulders heaving. Balling roots was a hard job, especially with no help. "I was hoping you'd reconsider my offer," he said.

"Not a chance."

He reached for his jacket, which he had tossed aside when exertion made him sweat. "It's a generous offer. You can make a new life somewhere else."

"I like it here."

He chuckled. "That won't last. Look at you—you're shaking with cold and it's only in the thirties. What are you going to do when the temperature drops below zero?"

Suddenly Jackie lost all patience. "Oh, for heaven's

sake, Sam. Give it a rest. You can't scare me into leaving with all your tales of gloom and doom. I know the weather is going to get bad…real bad. I also know I'm living at the edge of nowhere. I can't get pizza delivered and forget going back to bed with the Sunday paper. I know all that," she emphasized, "and I'm prepared to accept it, because it's the kind of life I want. Peaceful. Serene. Cozy. I'm going to spend the winter reading all the books I never had time to before and writing poetry. I'm looking forward to the solitude.

"The only thing I am not looking forward to," she added, swallowing against angry frustration, "is your hassling me about how I won't survive. So, read my lips—get off my back, okay?"

He held up a hand. "Hey, wait a minute. I've only been trying to tell you what you're in for. I don't want you to come crying to me when the going gets rough."

"Oh, Sam, when have I ever cried to you? Have I asked you to fix my leaky faucet or chop firewood? No. And I won't. I'm going to make it on my own, and it might just be with your attitude that I mean that literally come spring."

His eyes went wide as her meaning took hold. "You'd do that? You'd really try to run your half of the farm yourself?"

"Not try," she corrected. "I'll do it if I have to."

He snorted and shook his head, and, with hands on his hips stared down at her and said, "You're real cocky, aren't you? Think you know everything."

"Not yet. But I will." She glanced away. His shirt was unbuttoned halfway, and the sight of his broad, thickly matted chest was making her cheeks feel warm, and she was afraid he would notice. "Now what's on the schedule for tomorrow if it doesn't snow tonight? Are you going to plant seeds in the nursery?''

"No. The mulch trucks are scheduled to be here."

That was something new and she asked him to explain.

''They're trucks with special grinding machines. We feed in all the branches we've trimmed off, all the trash and so forth, to make mulch. We use it for the tender trees in the field that need a little protection from winter.''

She was surprised he did not have his own grinders and said so.

He shook his head at such a preposterous idea. ''A special truck like that would cost well over a hundred thousand dollars, Jackie. I hardly think there's enough mulching to be done around here to justify that kind of expense.'' He gestured to the truck. ''Let's go. You don't have any business being out here in this wind.''

Jackie looked at him long and hard and decided in that instant that even though he was drop-dead good-looking and, when he wanted to be, a heck of a lot of fun to be around, at that particular moment he was insufferable.

''I enjoy the wind,'' she snapped. ''Almost as much as I enjoy being by myself instead of with an old grump.''

She started walking toward the woods.

''Have it your way,'' he called. ''If you get lost, don't come whining to me.''

She kept on going. She was probably being childish, but so what? He had let her know, in dozens of ways, that he considered her an intruder, a nuisance, and wanted to get rid of her. So why should she care what he thought?

It was a long walk back to the cabin from where she had started at the barns and sheds. Had she begun from Sam's house, as Brian did when he slipped away, it would not be far at all. She knew because she had gone that way once out of curiosity. She told herself it wasn't spying, although she had tarried awhile to stare at the house and marvel over how pretty it was.

Two stories, gleaming white, with a red roof, it also had a railed porch that ran down two sides and across the front. Withered wisteria and honeysuckle vines clung tenaciously to the trellises. Asleep for the winter, she knew they would be glorious in the spring.

There was also a barn and a pasture. She could see a garden area that did not appear to have been worked lately, for it was thick with weeds. The clothesline was bare. And the house, overall, had a sad, neglected air about it. Curtains were drawn at all the windows. Flowerpots and hanging baskets on the porch had looked empty.

Somehow she knew the place had not always seemed so miserable and neglected. Generations before had probably had happy times—cookouts, picnics, children running and playing on the lawn. It had to have changed when Sam's wife had left. Or maybe when she came. Whatever or whenever, Jackie thought it was a terrible waste.

But she did not go that route when she left Sam, and it took her nearly an hour to get home.

She was exhausted—and also chilled to the bone.

The first thing she did was peel out of her clothes, fill the tub, then climb in to soak till the water was no longer warm.

Two cups of homemade soup from the crock pot, and

she was ready to curl up beneath the blankets on her bed and read till she couldn't hold her eyes open any longer.

She was exhausted and glad of it. That meant she was too tired to dream about Sam Colton—his dimpled smile, his strong, broad shoulders and how good he could make her feel when he was not in one of his bitter, cynical moods.

But when she awoke the next morning, she realized she had not been so tired after all.

Because she had spent the entire night with Sam.

In her dreams, anyway.

Sam waited in her driveway. He was cold, even with his layered clothing, but he did not like to keep the engine running. When you lived out so far, it was smart to save gas as much as possible...even though he kept small tanks for emergencies.

He was not about to blow the horn to bring Jackie out of her cabin, either. It was not quite eight o'clock, and he didn't want to seem anxious. Just neighborly. He would say he was passing by, checking on whether crews had left any trimmings to be mulched in her neck of the woods. That was all. And he thought he'd give her a lift to the work area since her car wasn't ready. He knew because he had called Allen Parsons at home the night before. Things were slow because of the holiday. He'd have it by noon, though. Sam had already made arrangements for Hank to take her into town to get it. He wasn't about to make the trip and start talk.

No, he checked himself, that was not the reason.

Hard as it was to admit, the truth was he did not want to be alone with her for that length of time. A five-minute ride to where the mulching would take place was one thing. Twenty minutes to town was another.

Okay, he thought with a wave of guilt, so he was a

coward. He was afraid he might do or say something to let her know his feelings for her were starting to be anything but neighborly.

Which was another reason he wished she would take his offer and leave.

Get out of Dodge, by damn.

Out of his life.

And his heart.

The woman was not his type, for Pete's sake. She was another Donna. City born and bred, thought it was a lark to move to the mountains. What was it she'd said she wanted to do? Write poetry. Yeah, that fit in with the image some folks had of life up here. Creative thoughts blossomed. Freedom to let your imagination flow. Donna had said she wanted to paint. Up till the time she met him, she said she'd known nothing but turmoil. She was ready for peace.

What a laugh.

A month after they were married she started her weekend trips to Atlanta. Six months later she was actually trying to get him to sell out the farm and move there.

The front door of the cabin opened, and Sam gratefully pulled himself from the miserable past.

Jackie saw him, blinked in disbelief, then gave him that wide, glowing smile that always made him want to smile back.

Hurrying down the steps, she came to his window, which he had rolled down at the sight of her.

When she spoke, frosty puffs came from her mouth in the frigid morning air. "What on earth are you doing here?"

"Just checking things out to see if I need to have the boys truck stuff over from here to be mulched. Get in. I thought you might like a ride."

She ran around the front of the truck. He leaned across to open the door for her.

"I don't believe you," she said when she got in.

He felt a twinge of worry. Surely he wasn't that obvious. "What do you mean?"

"You came hoping I wouldn't be here…that I'd got lost in the woods or a bear ate me."

He bit back a smile. "Bears are hibernating."

"But you were hoping I was lost," she playfully accused. "Go on. Admit it. You think your troubles would be over, but they wouldn't, because if anything were to happen to me, the land would go to Libby's favorite charity—the animal shelter in Durham."

It was his turn to tease. "Have you ever thought about becoming a deep-sea diver, Jackie? You wouldn't even need a tank, because I've never seen anyone who could talk as long as you do without taking a breath. And I know about the animal shelter being the next beneficiary. Your lawyer told me."

"I breathe," she assured, not about to let him get under her skin. "You just don't see me. You aren't observant enough. Besides, Mr. Burkhalter was Libby's lawyer. Not mine."

And in the same breath, she asked, "Did you find out anything about my car? I've got to go into town and make some phone calls, get some firewood brought out, call a plumber and raise Cain with the phone company to get some lines put in. Doggone it, it's time they realized we're civilized here and need to be in touch with the outside world."

She chattered on until they reached the work area and she bounded out of the truck and began talking to the mulch workers like they were old friends.

Sam watched her in amazement. He had to hand it to her. She was sure trying to fit in. It was just a shame she was wasting so much time and probably much of the profits she had coming to her. It had been a good year.

He thought, too, of how completely rude he had been to her on a number of occasions and how she had not let it throw her. She had snapped right back, and, though he would never admit it, she had put him in his place a time or two.

She even acted like she genuinely wanted to be his friend: only he knew better. She was using him to learn all she could about the farm. Then if she did ultimately stay, she wouldn't need him to take care of her share.

But he chided himself for even worrying about it. He had other problems—like his mother nagging him to send Brian to an institution. She did not think he was going to ever speak again, and she wanted Sam to get on with his life. She also bluntly said that it would not be fair to a new wife to have to take on the responsibility of a child with disabilities.

His mother had changed since she had remarried and moved to the city. She was no longer the apple-cheeked housewife and mother wearing a clean apron with cookies baking in the oven. Now she wore designer jeans and cashmere sweaters, followed a low-fat diet, worked out at a gym and had dropped forty pounds. She insisted she had loved her years on the farm but life went on—something she constantly urged him to realize.

Brian, she said, would be happier with his kind, and though Sam thought it was a cold way to put it, there were times when he wondered whether she might be right. But if he ever did agree to let Brian go, it would not be for the sake of a woman. In the first place, he had no intention of marrying again, and, if he did, it wouldn't be to a flatlander, for God's sake. He'd learned his lesson there.

So that was another reason he had to get crazy notions out of his head over Jackie Lundigan.

The morning passed swiftly. He was glad when it was time for Hank to take Jackie into town, but groaned out loud when he said Bonnie was making lunch for all of them at Sam's house where she was keeping an eye on Brian. The last thing Sam wanted was Jackie for a luncheon guest, but Hank issued the invitation before he could say anything. He didn't know of any way he could have gotten out of it, anyway, without raising eyebrows.

Jackie was tickled to death, and when Bonnie met them at the front door, Jackie hugged her and said, "This was so sweet of you. I'm starved, and—" she squealed to see Brian peeking around a corner "—I get to see my favorite little bandit."

Sam watched as she dropped to her knees to hug him. Brian merely stood there woodenly, as always, allowing her to put her arms about him but not responding.

Jackie chattered on as though nothing were wrong. She took his hand and led him into the dining room. "Sam, I love your house. Look at all these antiques."

"I never thought of any of it as antiques," he said, taking his place at the head of the table. "Just old furniture that's been in the family for years."

"Then you don't know antiques." She made sure Brian was seated right next to her, then continued to glance about with interest.

Bonnie served up hot tomato soup, sourdough crackers, and chicken salad sandwiches.

"Delicious," Jackie gushed. "You made the soup from home-canned tomatoes, didn't you?"

Bonnie beamed. "How can you tell?"

"My grandmother used to can her tomatoes. It's a flavor you don't get in the store-bought kind."

"Well, I'm glad you like it," Bonnie said. Then she turned to Sam. "I'm sorry about the pecan pie."

Sam couldn't help looking disappointed. She had promised to make him one after he told how his mother refused to have any fattening desserts for Thanksgiving dinner now that she was on her health kick.

"I burned it," Bonnie apologized. "I got busy ironing the tablecloth and forgot it. I'm sorry."

"Don't worry about it," he said, smiling to let her know he was not upset. "Willa makes pecan pies this time of year. I'll just have to stop in at the Book Nook and see if it's my lucky day."

When they finished eating, Bonnie took Brian upstairs for his nap, and Hank asked Sam if there was anything he needed from town.

"Yeah, as a matter of fact there is," Sam said. "Tom called last night and said the seeds I ordered came in. That's good timing, because I'm going to spend the rest of the afternoon getting the beds ready in the nursery so I can start first thing tomorrow. If you could pick them up for me, I'll appreciate it."

"Will do." Hank took his hat from the rack near the door and shook it at Sam, "But you better make sure you've got that stove ready to fire up in the nursery. I don't care whether you can smell it or not, I say snow will be here by the weekend."

Sam walked to the door and told Jackie, "Take the rest of the day off. There's no need for you to come back. All I'm going to be doing is raking beds, and any rookie can do that."

"Ah, so now I'm a rookie." She laughed and caught Hank's arm. "Come on, before he really starts calling me names, although I think Bonnie's tomato soup has mellowed him a bit. He hasn't said one nasty thing in the last half hour."

"Oh, he's not so bad when you get to know him," Hank said, also laughing as they went on out.

Sam closed the door after them and told the nagging voice within to shut up for a few minutes. Being around Jackie always lifted his spirits somehow, and he wanted to savor the moment.

It was, after all, the first time since the trouble with Donna that the house had seemed like a nice, happy place to be.

If only for a little while.

It was nearly dark when Sam got back to the house. Bonnie had been watching for him and was ready to leave the minute he walked in.

"I'm sorry I'm late," he said, "but when Hank got back with those seeds, I decided to get a few trays planted."

"It's okay. Brian is watching TV. He's had his supper and will probably fall asleep on the couch. You've got leftovers from lunch, and I'm late for my circle meeting. See you tomorrow.

"Oh, almost forgot," she stopped halfway out the door. "There's a pecan pie on the table. It looks wonderful."

Sam broke into a wide grin. "Hey, you made another one. Thanks a lot."

"Oh, I didn't make it." She breezed on out, and he almost missed hearing her say, "Jackie did."

He hurried into the kitchen, and, sure enough, there was a crisp, golden brown pecan pie sitting on the counter. The smell of toasted nuts, butter and hot syrup was more than he could stand, and he immediately cut himself a slice.

It was delicious.

But as he ate, he couldn't help wondering about

Jackie's motive. Did she think if she got on the good side of him he would be more cooperative about teaching her what she needed to know so she could take over her half of the farm sooner?

Then he saw the envelope propped against the salt and pepper shakers.

He tore it open, pulse racing, his mind automatically going back to another time when he had read a note that turned his life to ashes.

He told himself to calm down. She had made him a pie, that's all. It wasn't a goodbye gift, and so what if it was? If she was leaving, whether she took his offer or not, well, it was for the best, and...

He began to read.

Hi Sam,
I saw how you tried not to show how disappointed you were at lunch today when Bonnie told you she'd burned your pie. So it gave me the idea for the perfect "happy" for you, so, here 'tis.
A "happy," by the way, is something you give to someone for no other reason than to make them happy—because they made you happy, like you did me, today, when you allowed me to come into your home and share lunch.
Enjoy

Jackie

He folded the note and put it away, then settled down to finish enjoying his pie. Somehow, it tasted all the better to know it wasn't a goodbye gift, after all.

Chapter Ten

Jackie couldn't wait to get to the nursery the next morning to hear how Sam had liked the pecan pie. She'd had to force herself not to leave any earlier than she did, afraid her eagerness would be obvious.

When she had gone to his house late the day before, Bonnie had been tickled pink when she'd seen the pie. It was his favorite, she'd said, and swore no one could make one like his mother. Well, Jackie wasn't trying to compete with Mrs. Colton, but she had been told more than once that hers could win a blue ribbon at the state fair.

She had learned to layer when she dressed—tank top, T-shirt, sweater and insulated vest. If it was very cold, as it was this morning, she also wore a heavy down jacket. But it would be warm inside the nursery, and she could start peeling down. Sam, it seemed, had to really be cold to wear more than a flannel shirt, which he seldom buttoned all the way up.

She wondered if he knew what a terrific body he had. His jeans looked like they'd been molded to his nice, round buttocks. But she doubted he gave much thought to his personal appearance at all, other than cleanliness. He wasn't the type. His good looks just came naturally, and if he was aware of being a hunk, he didn't let on.

Jackie figured he actually didn't care. He had a son everyone was trying to make him believe was retarded and a huge farm to run. He also had her to worry about—only he didn't realize yet that it wasn't necessary. He thought it was all a lark to her, unwilling to accept the fact that it was actually her life.

The hothouse was a long, narrow building situated not far behind Sam's house. It had been built on level ground, which was, of course, not easy to find in the mountainous terrain. An electric heater stood outside the door. Sam had told her it had cost a small fortune to install, and he hadn't been able to do it till after his father died. The elder Colton had been a real penny-pincher and used a corn furnace to warm the nursery. It did not work well in sub-zero temperatures, and sometimes valuable seedlings were lost. Sam put in a state-of-the art system with a backup generator.

Jackie had wondered about another hothouse she'd seen, on her land, not far from the cabin. It looked as though it had been used a long time ago, and when she asked Sam, he said it had been abandoned after his was modernized.

"If you go over the records your lawyer has probably given you, you'll see part of the cost of upgrading was deducted from Libby's share of the profits that year. But she never questioned it. I guess she had so much money she didn't notice…or care.''

"That wasn't the case,'' Jackie had informed him with a touch of indignity over the slight at Libby. "Didn't any of you Coltons ever realize that the reason you didn't hear from her was that she just didn't want to make waves? All she wanted was to have something to remember Roy Colton by—his land. The money wasn't important, so she wouldn't have given a rat's fanny how much you spent on improvements.''

That had ended the conversation, which was a good thing. As much as Jackie wanted to get along with him, she would not stand for any criticism of Libby.

Hank's truck was parked outside the nursery, but Sam's was nowhere around.

"Good morning,'' she called, opening the door and immediately starting to unzip her jacket. It was warm to the point of sweltering, after coming in from the frigid air outside.

"Mornin', Jackie,'' Hank said from where he was already at work making little indentions with a small scoop in a seed tray.

Jackie loved the nursery with its loamy, woodsy smell. And she liked strolling down the aisles to see the different stages of development, from the newly planted seedbeds to the nearly two-year-old seedlings that would be transplanted to the fields in the spring.

By the time she had walked up and down the rows, she was hot enough to have to take off her down vest. Hank was working in a T-shirt, sweat on his brow. She asked him where Sam was. "He's usually the first one at work.''

"Beats me,'' Hank said with a shrug. "He said he had some things to do that might take most of the morning. Maybe longer. Must have been important, though I didn't ask. I never ask. Sam's pretty closemouthed about his business, especially since his wife left. He don't have much to say to nobody, but at least he didn't turn retarded like his boy.''

Jackie bit back the angry impulse to tell him Brian had not turned retarded for heaven's sake. She did not want to alienate him. She wanted to hear as much as he was willing to tell.

Positioning herself on the other side of the dirt-filled trays, she began to make holes for the seeds. ''I guess that was pretty awful.''

''Yeah. But not because he cared anything about her, mind you. It was the boy. Brian was torn all to pieces. I mean, when you think about her walking out on him in the middle of the night.'' He shook his head to think.

Jackie was aghast and begged him to tell her everything. Hank liked to talk and was eager to describe that fateful night when Brian wound up making his way through the woods to find his father after his mother deserted him.

As Jackie listened, she worked furiously, blinking back tears to think of how awful it must have been for him.

Hank said Sam wasn't all that surprised. ''I think he knew she'd take off sooner or later. It just threw him that she could abandon the boy.''

Jackie worked even harder, planting twice as many seeds as Hank did. Then he noticed and said, ''Hey, you're puttin' 'em too deep. They'll never sprout.''

She apologized and, embarrassed, started over.

Hank finished his section and looked at his watch. ''It's ten o'clock, and Bonnie is never late, so I'd say right about now—''

The door to the hothouse opened, and Bonnie walked in with a thermos of coffee and a bag of brownies and chocolate chip cookies still warm from the oven.

"I knew it," he said with a grin, hugging her before taking the goodies she'd brought.

Then Jackie saw Brian, coming right behind Bonnie. He walked right over to her and climbed up on the empty stool beside her.

"Well, would you look at that?" Bonnie cried. "He won't have anything to do with me, but he sure has taken a shine to you."

Jackie gave him a hug. He did not respond, merely sat there woodenly, watching her with big, sad eyes. She offered him a brownie, but he continued to stare, not bothering to even shake his head to decline.

"Sometimes I wonder if he can hear," Hank mused as he munched on a cookie. "He doesn't act like he knows a thing that's said to him."

"Oh, he knows, all right," Bonnie said. "He's just stubborn, that's all. But I agree with Mrs. Colton that he needs to be sent off to one of those schools for his kind. It's not good for him not to be around other kids, and he can't start school next year the way he is now. Sam is going to have to do it, whether he wants to or not." She punctuated with a loud sigh.

Jackie was not going to waste time arguing with them. But she was going to raise the subject with Sam again.

Then she remembered the pie. "Did he like it?" she asked Bonnie.

"I guess so. Looks like he ate two pieces last night. He didn't say anything about it this morning." She pursed her lips and thought about it. "In fact, he was acting kind of funny. He was on the phone in his office when I got there, and he talked to somebody a long time.

Then when he came out he said he had to go somewhere and took off.''

"Yeah. He wouldn't even tell me,'' Hank said.

When they had finished their coffee, Bonnie told Brian it was time for them to go back to the house.

He sat right where he was, watching Jackie as she went back to planting seeds, and made no move to get down off the stool.

Bonnie raised her voice a bit. "Brian, I said let's go.''

Brian ignored her.

"Maybe you'd better go with her,'' Jackie leaned to say to him when she saw Bonnie was getting angry. "She might not let you come out here with her next time.''

At that he got down off the stool.

"See?'' Jackie looked from Bonnie to Hank proudly. "There's nothing wrong with his hearing. He just didn't want to go, that's all.''

Bonnie pushed him gently out the door, then turned to say, "Well, he's sure taken a shine to you. It's a shame Sam don't want him having anything to do with you.''

"He told you that?'' Jackie asked, stunned.

"He sure did. He said he didn't want him to be upset when you leave.''

"And he's sure I will,'' Jackie said testily.

Bonnie shrugged. "Well, you're a flatlander, like Donna was. I guess he thinks—''

"I guess,'' Jackie cut her off, unable to contain her annoyance any longer, "that Sam Colton thinks he knows everything.''

Bonnie and Hank exchanged looks Jackie did not see. Her head was bent over her work, hands trembling.

"Well, see you at lunch,'' Bonnie said, leaving.

"Brownies and cookies are enough for me," Jackie said tightly. She was not about to go back to the house for lunch, not after Sam had so rudely left without taking time to drop by the hothouse to say thanks for the pie. He was an ungrateful clod, and he was also insensitive to his son's needs. There was nothing wrong with Brian wanting to be with her, even if she were to leave one day.

The day wore on. Hank went for lunch, then returned. They made small talk about things that had to do with the farm. She asked him questions about the trees, wanting to learn as much as possible. After all, it looked as though it would be in her best interest to branch off from Sam and run her own business.

So what if they would be in competition with each other? She had read that the wholesale sales of the North Carolina tree industry the year before had topped a hundred million dollars. After all, the state produced over 15 percent of all the real Christmas trees in the United States. And Fraser firs represented over 90 percent of all species grown in the state. She had plenty on her land. She would do fine. All she had to do was learn the ins and outs, and then she would not need Sam Colton, by golly. Maybe she would even plant trees across the road in front to cut him off from her land.

And fences. She would have lots of fences. She would let him know what was hers. She'd have a new survey done, too, and—

"You're diggin' too deep again, Jackie."

She threw down the scoop. "Maybe I'd better call it a day."

"Just as I thought," Sam boomed as he opened the door in time to hear Jackie. "I turn my back and everybody wants to quit for the day."

Jackie could not resist saying, "Seems to me you haven't even started."

"That's what you think." He glanced about at the seed beds they had completed and nodded with satisfaction. "I have to say you all got a lot done. We'll take the next couple of days off, then next week we'll do some shearing on the trees that will be ready to harvest next year.

"And you're right," he said to Jackie. "It is time to call it a day. By the way, thanks for the pie."

He walked on out, and she felt like scooping up a handful of dirt from the seedbed and throwing it at him. She had worked hard on the pie. The crust had been one of her best, just the right amount of butter to make it flaky yet tender. But he acted like it was no big deal. Then she decided she was probably overreacting. What did she expect, anyway? That he would come rushing in and give her a hug and a kiss?

It would have been nice, though, wouldn't it? a little voice within teased.

She grimaced against it and pulled her sweater over her head. When Sam had opened the door she had felt the frigid temperature, so it was time to start layering her clothing again before plunging out in it.

"See you in a couple of days, Hank," she called on her way out. "Actually, I'm glad we aren't working. I've got to round up some firewood."

He was spreading plastic over the beds they had just seeded for additional warmth and humidity. "Hey, why didn't you say something earlier? I'll call Seth Barwick when I get up to the house and tell him you need a load first thing tomorrow. Will half a cord do it?"

"Wait and let me see how much I can afford. I might find some stacked in one of the outbuildings. I sure hope so, because I still think we're going to get snow soon, even if Sam can't smell it.''

''Wouldn't be surprised. Just make sure you've got a lot of groceries. Water, too, in case your pipes freeze.''

''I'll be fine, Hank. Actually, I'm looking forward to it. I've got enough fixing for hot chocolate and marshmallows to last till spring.''

''Hey, great,'' he said and laughed. ''If Bonnie runs out, I'll put on my cross-country skis and pay you a visit.''

Jackie's eyes went wide at the sight of firewood stacked neatly at the side of the house. It was a cord, at least.

It could only have been Sam's doing. He had taken it upon himself to have it delivered.

But no.

She came to an abrupt halt on her way inside. A brand-new ax was propped against the chopping block. Had Sam chopped the wood himself?

Shivering against the cold, she hurried inside. Then, on a hunch, went to the kitchen corner and opened the cabinet under the sink.

It was bone dry.

He had fixed the leak.

She felt like dancing, and, actually did so, whirling around and around, hugging herself with delight to think that Sam Colton, despite all his gruffness, was really a nice guy.

Then she saw the note she had missed before, propped on the table between the salt and pepper shakers.

Snatching it up, she read:

The pie made me happy, so I thought I'd pass on a few happies of my own to say thanks. So now we're even.

By the way, the phone company will start running lines next week...if it doesn't snow.

Sam

She stared at the note for a long, long time, and though she was grateful for what he had done, one line kept leaping out at her.

So now we're even.

Was that all it meant to him to chop her wood, fix her faucet and pull some strings to get her phone line put in? A payback for a pecan pie? That wasn't the way "happies" were meant to be at all. They were given as an expression of joy given and received but never an obligation.

But Sam, she feared, was just too soured on life to see it that way.

Dawn was gray, like whispery fingers clawing to find sunshine, but none was to be found.

Jackie stepped onto the front porch, pulling her wool bathrobe around her and thought maybe she smelled snow...not that she was sure what it smelled like. But something was in the air—fresh, biting, pungent. And the clouds were the color of gunmetal, strong and foreboding.

She checked the temperature. Thirty-one degrees. Perfect for the white stuff, all right.

After putting on jeans and jacket, she brought in several armloads of wood to stack near the stove. Remembering that she'd seen a tarpaulin in one of the storage sheds, she got that and spread it across the rest of the wood to keep it dry.

She checked her supplies. Canned goods. Bottled water. Candles. Matches. She had everything she needed. "Let it snow, let it snow, let it snow," she sang out loud.

Now if only it were Christmas, she thought, then remembered she had not even thought about a tree for herself. In fact, it had slipped her mind that this would be her very first Christmas alone, with no one to share it with. The year before she had still been married, but in name only. She did not see Kevin all through the holidays. He had offered no explanation, and she hadn't asked for one, assuming he was working. Now she suspected otherwise, but it made no difference, because she no longer cared. And probably hadn't then, either, only she didn't realize it at the time. The season had been enjoyable, though, even without a husband or family to share it with. She had gladly put in extra time at Dove Haven, baking and decorating cookies, cakes, even making a real gingerbread house to put in the lobby for the residents and their guests to enjoy.

So it had been a rewarding time, and she vowed then and there to make contact with a nursing home in the area so she could again feel like she was bringing a little joy into people's lives.

And maybe by doing so she could put some into her own, as well.

The television reception was not very good. She managed to hear the weather forecast. Snow was coming, all right. Ten to twelve inches was predicted for the higher elevations. The ski resorts were ecstatic, but everyone else was bracing for the inconveniences sure to come— hazardous driving conditions, power outages, school closings.

Jackie was a bit nervous. It would be her first-ever

snow storm. Sure, the Durham area had gotten a few inches from time to time over the years, but nothing major and it usually didn't last long. But this was different. It was also serious. She could be snowed in for days. Sam wouldn't check on her. He had made sure she had enough firewood. It was up to her to take care of the rest. He had warned her it could get rough and would be gloating when it did, hoping it would make her leave.

She made a beef stew, filling the crock pot with chunks of meat, potatoes, carrots and onions. The smell made her mouth water. It would simmer all afternoon, and the gravy would be so thick and delicious she would have to make fat, fluffy baking powder biscuits to eat with it.

In mid-afternoon sleet began falling. That was bad, because it meant ice would be under the snow, making it much more treacherous to be out in.

She curled up on the sofa near the fireplace and wrapped up in an afghan. She started reading, but it was all too cozy with the ice pellets striking the tin roof so melodiously. Soon she was fast asleep.

The next thing she knew someone was tugging at the afghan, and her eyes flashed open to see Brian standing beside her.

She sat up quickly. "Honey, what are you doing here?"

Then she saw he was pointing toward the window, and she was not sure which overwhelmed the most—the fact that he was actually trying to tell her something for the first time or that it was snowing like crazy.

"Would you look at that," she said, awed, as he took her hand and drew her to the window.

The flakes were big and coming down so hard it was hard to see out. They were sticking, too. The ground looked as though it was already covered in several inches.

She hugged him to her. "Oh, Brian, you shouldn't be here. I'm glad to see you, little guy, but you know your daddy said you couldn't go off in the woods by yourself. Now what am I going to do with you?"

He gave no indication of having heard her and ran to the door and flung it open.

Jackie came up behind him and saw that the snow was blowing and had also covered the porch.

Then it dawned.

There were no footprints in the snow. Not on the porch. Not in the yard. "How did you get it?" she wondered aloud. The back door was latched, because it kept popping open, and she was afraid raccoons would invite themselves in. So Brian had to have come in the front door, which meant he had been there awhile.

Taking his hand and pulling him inside, she closed the door against the storm. Then, returning to the living area, she noticed how he had made himself a bed on the shaggy rug in front of the sofa. Probably he had been napping while she also snoozed.

And when she went into the kitchen to offer him a biscuit she discovered that he had already quietly helped himself.

"Little bandit," she said lovingly, ruffling his hair.

He pressed his head against her side, and her heart gave a leap. He was showing his affection, and she was deeply touched. "I like you too, sweetie," she said, her arm going around him to squeeze him tight.

"But," she said with worried sigh, "what am I going to do with you? We can't walk in this weather, and the snow is too deep for me to drive in as worn out as my tires are. We'd wind up in a ditch for sure and be stuck till your daddy comes looking for you.''

She snapped her fingers.

''That's it. We'll just let him come looking, which he will do the second Bonnie realizes you're missing. What did you do? Sneak out while she thought you were napping?''

She gently gripped his shoulder and bent down so she could look straight into his eyes. Maybe he wasn't able to speak, but the eyes of a child do not lie, and she could tell she'd hit the nail on the head. That meant Bonnie would be checking on him soon and finding him missing. Then she'd have to find Sam to let him know, and Sam, of course, would know right where to look.

''Tell you what we'd better do,'' Jackie said. ''Your daddy is going to be real mad, so we'll try to get on his good side by having a nice meal waiting for him. How's that?''

Brian's expression did not change but she thought she saw a teeny flash of approval.

''Let's see.'' She tapped a finger to her chin. ''I'll make more biscuits, and you can keep watch and let me know when you see his headlights okay? The minute you do, I'll put them in the oven.''

To her amazement, he got down off the stool he had been sitting on, dragged it over to the window, then climbed up on it again to begin his vigil.

There was no way that child was retarded, and it made Jackie furious to think anyone could even hint that he was. And as soon as her phone was put in, she was going to start making some phone calls. Through working at the rest home, and marriage to someone studying to be a doctor, she had made a few contacts in the medical field and intended to use them to see what she could learn about Brian's condition.

She was busy rolling out biscuit dough and lost in thought when Brian suddenly began tugging at her apron. She looked out the window but didn't see any headlights, and just then there was a hard pounding on the door.

She opened it, and there stood Sam. He looked like a walking snowman. "What on earth…"

"I had an accident." He brushed by her and saw Brian and said with overwhelming relief, "Thank God. I thought he'd be here, but I couldn't be sure."

"What kind of accident?" Jackie prodded, worried he might be hurt. "Are you okay?"

"Oh, I'm all right. I just hit a patch of ice under the snow and slid off the road and hooked up with a fence. I couldn't get the truck out, and I couldn't raise anybody on the CB to come help. I guess everybody's home by the fire—where they should be," he added pointedly with a glower at Brian. "So I had to walk almost all the way here, and believe me, it was no picnic."

Jackie hated that he'd had such a bad time. "Listen, get those wet clothes off. I'll dry them by the fire. You can wrap up in that afghan over there. Then have some supper, and we'll figure out what to do. One thing's for certain, Brian can't walk home in this."

She hurried back to her biscuits. "You can undress in the bedroom." She grimaced. He must think she was a real bimbo to suggest he would've stripped right where he stood unless she instructed him otherwise.

A few moments later she heard the wet plop of his things as they hit the floor. She picked them up and draped them over the back of a chair she'd positioned near the heat.

"They should dry in no time. That's a roaring fire."

"And whatever you're cooking smells wonderful. Beef stew?" He sniffed.

She was kneading the dough but turned to tell him he had guessed right. That was when she saw him standing there, the afghan wrapped around his waist. With his damp hair tumbling about his face, arms folded across his bare chest and firm, muscular legs spread apart, it was all she could do to keep from gasping out loud. He looked so sexy and appealing that she gulped, swallowed and spun back to the counter so fast she hit the flour bowl, sending a white cloud into her face.

She sneezed.

"Bless you."

"Thank you," she whispered, then, clearing her throat said, "And thanks, also, for what you did today—fixing the faucet, making arrangements to have phone lines run out here. And if you hadn't chopped all that firewood, I'd be in a mess tonight with this storm."

"And so would I," he said cheerily. "Seeing how I wound up here. It's nice to get warm before plunging out in that mess again."

She hated the thought of him having to, but wasn't about to say so. She didn't want it to appear that she was happy over his predicament...although she was.

"Well, it's really appreciated," she said.

"Glad to do it. Call it a happy." He grinned.

Quiet moments passed, then, with a thoughtful look at Brian, Sam murmured, "So I'll have another talk with him about not sneaking off, and it won't do any more good than all the others, because sometimes I don't think he understands a word I say."

"Yes, he does." She told him how he'd kept watch for him after she told him to. "He let me know you were on the porch. I left the light on, and he saw you when he was waiting for your truck.''

''I don't know.'' He sat down at the table. ''It's beyond me. I hate to punish him. He's been through so much.''

''Let me think on all this, Sam.'' She slid the pan of biscuits into the oven. ''I know some people. Let me ask questions.''

''Thanks, Jackie, but my mother has taken him to the best doctors money can buy.''

She decided to let the subject drop for the time being and took two wineglasses from a cabinet. They had been a wedding gift, but she hadn't tossed them. No need to give up good crystal.

She also had a nice bottle of wine that she had been saving for a special occasion. She remembered asking a friend once how a person could tell when that time came. And her friend had answered, ''Believe me, you'll know.''

And she did.

And this was it.

She poured them each a glass.

Sam took a sip and smiled. ''Burgundy. My favorite. California?''

''Sure is. It's my favorite, too.''

He took another sip, leaned back and closed his eyes. ''I'm going to enjoy every drop of this, and I'll think about it when I'm walking home in ankle-deep snow.''

But Sam and Jackie were not paying any attention to what was going on in the winter wonderland outside. They were too engrossed in wine, good food…and each other.

They didn't know that the snow was coming down even harder.

And it was way beyond ankle deep.

Chapter Eleven

"I haven't seen him eat like that in quite a while," Sam said as he watched Brian finish a second helping of stew. "But then I'm not as good a cook as you are. Neither is Bonnie, I'm afraid."

Jackie demurely thanked him, basking in his praise as he poured them another glass of wine.

"I guess your husband misses your cooking." Then, seeing how she frowned, apologized. "I'm sorry. I didn't mean to bring up bad memories."

"Hey, it's okay." She was quick to put him at ease. "The fact is, Kevin didn't like eating at home. I can't tell you the number of times he would walk out on a meal I'd cooked to go eat in a restaurant with some of his friends. He was a real social animal. Always wanting to be seen with the right people."

"So what did you do?"

"Once I became dietician at the rest home, I'd help

with the cooking there.'' Her lips curved in a bitter smile. ''It gave me something to do while my marriage fell apart. I spent more time there than I did at home, which made no difference since Kevin was never around, anyway. That's how I became close friends with some of the residents.

''Like Libby Pratt,'' she added. It still rankled that he had practically accused her of manipulating Libby into leaving her in her will.

He was quiet for a moment, and she knew he had got the point when he said, ''Well, I can see how friendships like that get forged. She was alone, and so were you.''

''I never knew about the land, Sam, till after she was gone. You have to believe that.''

He held up a hand in capitulation, reaching for his wineglass with his other. ''I do believe it.'' He took a quick sip. ''And I'm sorry I ever thought otherwise, but you have to agree it came as a shock. But what's done is done.''

''You mean you've accepted the fact I'm here to stay?''

He looked her straight in the eye. ''I've accepted the fact that you think you are.''

''Then what about Brian?''

Sam looked at his son, who was polishing off a huge slice of pecan pie covered in whipped cream. ''What about him?''

''Are you still going to forbid him to come to see me?''

Sam took a big sip of wine before saying, ''I'm afraid so. Maybe it is a clear path from my house to here, and it would probably be okay if he didn't wander off it, but the fact remains that I don't want him to get attached to you, Jackie. Come spring and you decide you can't cut it and want to sell out to me—or continue like Libby did and just collect your share of the profits—I don't want him hurt by having someone else in his life disappear.''

She waited until Brian got up from the table and went to sit on the sofa. Then she lowered her voice and said, ''I understand your reason but not your logic, especially when you're considering sending him away.''

''Not before spring.''

''Well, I won't encourage him,'' she said finally, ''but as I've told you before, I won't run him off.''

''Then Bonnie will just have to keep a better watch. I'll also put a lock on his door.''

Jackie cleared the table, then brought coffee and pie for both of them.

They talked about things concerning the farm for awhile. Then the coffee mugs were empty…along with the wine bottle. There were a few moments of awkward silence, and Jackie was beginning to suspect that maybe Sam just didn't want to leave. But that didn't mean he liked her company that much. After all, it was a nasty night out, and he had a long walk ahead of him.

Finally he stood. ''Well, this has been nice, Jackie.''

He had pulled the afghan up to his shoulders while he ate but let it drape back down around his hips. Her pulse started racing again, and she knew if she did not get busy washing dishes or doing something, he was going to see how the sight of his naked chest was affecting her.

''What…what about Brian?'' she asked, hardly trusting her voice to speak. He was sound asleep on the sofa.

''I guess I have no choice but to leave him here for the night if you don't mind.''

''Of course I don't,'' she said softly and went to tuck

a blanket around him. "You'd have a fight on your hands if you tried to leave here with him walking in this weather."

"Well, it's probably stopped snowing by now, anyway." He went to the door, opened it, and promptly cried, "Oh, my God."

"What is it?" Jackie rushed to look and repeated his stunned exclamation, hand flying to her mouth. The snow was almost waist high.

"Dammit, it must be three feet, and it's still coming down. That's the problem up here. Despite weather forecasts, we never know how bad it's going to be, because the elevation is so high. Anything can happen."

An awkward silence descended, as neither knew what to say, because it was obvious Sam could not walk home.

Jackie drew a nervous breath so deep it went to the pit of her stomach, and she let it out in a rush. "Well, I can take Brian to bed with me, and you can sleep on the sofa. Then in the morning, we can figure out what to do."

"Oh, in the daylight I can make it. There's a pair of snowshoes in one of those storage sheds out back unless you got on a cleaning kick and threw them out."

"No. They're still there. I remember seeing them when I was checking things out to see if it would make a good hen house."

"Hen house?" he echoed with an incredulous laugh. "You've got to be kidding. You can't have chickens up here unless you go to the expense of a heater. What would you do on a night like this? Invite them to dinner like you did me?"

Jackie had already realized it was not feasible, but joined Sam in laughing about the foolishness of such a notion. It lightened the tension that had wrapped about them.

"Well, I'll get the kitchen cleaned up, and you can move Brian to my bed. I doubt he'll wake up."

Her hands were shaking as she ran hot water in the sink and poured in liquid detergent. It was so terribly unnerving to think that Sam was going to sleep in the next room, and no doubt in the nude, too, and—

She clapped her hands together in the suds to dispel such thoughts, sending a spray of tiny bubbles flying to her face and making her sneeze.

"Bless you."

She jumped.

He was standing beside her, the afghan still draped around his waist, only he had not realized it had dropped a few inches.

Her eyes had a will of their own, gaze lowering to trail the thick mat of hair on his chest tapering to his navel and below.

He saw her staring and yanked up the afghan. "Sorry. I was about to look like a male stripper and didn't know it."

"You'd make a good one," she blurted out, instantly wanting to cram her fist in her mouth. She had no right to make such a remark, for goodness sake, especially under the circumstances. It was the wine talking, because she was feeling so mellow, so relaxed. It was also the ambience of the situation, as well. Cozy and warm inside. A winter wonderland outside. And a Kenny G CD playing to fill the air with soft, sensuous music.

For a moment neither spoke.

Jackie thought about apologizing for her remark, but decided that would just prolong the awareness that had sprung between them.

She also thought about getting back to washing the dishes, but, try as she might, she could not tear her locked gaze from Sam's blue eyes.

He found his voice first. "That's a compliment. Thanks." His smile was wry. "But I'm not really a good dancer."

"I—I'm not either," she managed to say past the lump in her throat.

"Maybe—" he moved closer "—we could learn together."

She stepped into his arms without thinking about it, and they began moving slowly to the rhythm of the music.

His hand moved farther down her back, firm, caressing, as he pulled her closer still.

She was wearing a lounge outfit made of pink velour and no bra beneath. She had high, firm breasts, and straps made her uncomfortable. Besides, she had not been expecting company, did not know she would wind up with a dinner date.

Her chest pressed against his, and she felt her nipples grow hard. Frantically she wondered if he could feel them against his bare skin. She tried to pull back, but he held her tight.

Her eyes were level with his chin, but she would not look up at him...did not want him to see how her cheeks had to be flaming, for heat was coursing through her body like a mountain stream running wild.

His warm fingers laced through hers, his thumb making circles on her palm that sent tantalizing needles into her spine.

Gently, as natural as breathing, she turned her head to rest on his broad shoulder.

He hugged her even closer; not a pin could have been placed between them.

And then she felt it—his hardened manhood pressing against her.

He did not pull back.

Neither did she.

They continued to dance, taking small, sometimes clumsy steps, but always they clung together, never backing away for even an instant.

Jackie did not at first realize how she had turned her mouth to brush his flesh. When she did, she continued, lips nuzzling ever so lightly.

She felt him kiss her forehead and shivered to the tips of her toes.

Never in her whole life had a man made her feel this way. She found herself praying the music would never end, that they could stay in each other's arms all through eternity.

His hand slipped beneath her shirt, his touch hot like fire on her already steaming body.

With his other hand, he cupped her face, devouring her for an instant with his eyes before closing his mouth over hers.

He tasted of warm, sweet wine, and she boldly parted his lips with her tongue to enjoy the erotic zest all the more.

His hands moved around to gently knead her breasts as though sampling fruit for ripeness. Then he squeezed each nipple between thumb and forefinger, like plucking a sweet cherry, then rolling, only to pull, pluck, then pinch ever so lightly, ever so sweetly.

Her knees threatened to buckle.

He felt it and held her up and against him.

The tips of their tongues met, hungrily teasing, then

devouring greedily as though they could not get enough of each other.

She clung to him as he moved his lips to trail down her neck.

They were no longer dancing.

He pressed her back against the sink and deftly lifted her shirt, exposing her breasts.

Her head fell backward, neck arching, as she offered herself to him, breath harsh, heaving, in anticipation.

Fire exploded in her chest as his lips dove to fasten around one nipple and suck hard, then soft, then repeating again and again, suckling, tasting, devouring. Ever so lightly, then roughly sucking as much of her as he could take into his mouth, again and again, nibbling, licking.

Jackie was dizzy. Her own hands began to move. Up and down his back. Nails slightly raking. Her hips began to undulate.

And then she touched where the afghan rolled at his waist. Without hesitation, she pulled it apart, and it fell to the floor.

He kicked it out of the way and pressed himself into her, then pulled back long enough to hook his thumbs in the waist of her slacks and yank them down.

Cupping her bottom, he lifted her to stand on her toes as he slid his shaft between her thighs.

To and fro, he rubbed again and again, touching the nucleus of her sex and sending hot daggers of fire into her belly.

Kevin had been the only man who had ever made love to her, but never, ever, like this.

Heaven and hell rolled into one as a part of her screamed for fulfillment and another whispered to back away lest he take her heart along with her body.

Boldly, she reached for him, softly, tenderly. And even as he continued to stroke himself between her legs, she ran her fingertips up and down his manhood.

She marveled at the size of him.

He was huge.

She wondered if she could take all of him, but knew she had to find out.

Her hips began to undulate once more, and she moved from caressing him to clinging to his shoulders instead. Weakness from want made her afraid she could not continue to stand.

"Tell me that you want me," he whispered, breath burning into her neck as he bent her back over the sink. "Or tell me to stop...."

She could more easily have moved the mountains they called home than deny him...or herself, and, for answer, reached down and guided him inside her.

He grasped her waist, lifting her up and onto him, and she strained on tiptoe to slide up and down the rigid shaft. She moaned softly to feel the girth of him.

He drew back. "Am I hurting you?" He searched her face.

She clutched his shoulders, pulling him closer, wanting all of him. "No, no. I want all of you..."

He laughed, deep and throaty. "Then you shall have me, my sweet."

He lifted her up, still impaling her and carried her to the sofa. She held on tight, wrapping her arms around him tightly, raining kisses all over his face.

She was wanton.

She was wild.

And she didn't care.

To hell with tomorrow and anything else, because she

felt in that instant if she did not have him she would surely die from want.

He started to lay her on the sofa.

"No. There." She pointed to the faux fur rug in front of the fireplace. She had splurged and ordered it from a catalog the same day she made the decision to move to the mountains. She'd imagined lying on it sipping hot chocolate, never dreaming she'd know the delicious feel of it against her naked flesh while a man made her realize what it truly meant to be a woman.

Never had she felt so uninhibited, and, oh, it was wonderful, she sighed to think as she wriggled against the rug.

Sam lowered himself onto her. She spread her legs to receive him, but he toyed with her instead. With his eyes burning into hers, he spread the petals of her sex and began to stroke.

Jackie squirmed as he began to manipulate the tiny nub hidden within, making it swell beneath his massaging fingers.

She twisted from side to side, then fastened her hands around his wrist to try and stop the sweet torture. "No, please. I can't stand it. I've got to have you now…"

"And you will." He smiled down at her, enjoying her torment as much as she. He wanted the magic to last, wanted to ensure that when the final moment of ecstasy came, that pinnacle of sensory emotion, they would fly to that wondrous peak together.

He lowered his mouth to suckle her breast again, and she clung to him, arms wrapped around his neck, trying to bring him closer.

She reached for his manhood and gently pulled it toward her, beckoning, begging.

At last he reached his point of surrender but drew back

to worriedly say, "Jackie, I don't have anything…you know…with me. Is it safe?"

She whispered that it was, not bothering to explain her doctor had put her on birth control pills to regulate her periods. But in that frenzied moment she doubted she would have cared and thrown caution to the wind in order to have him.

Grasping her hips, he plunged into her.

She cried out, "Yes…oh, yes…" and lifted her buttocks to receive him. She raised her legs, wrapped them about him, her heels tucked against his buttocks.

She could not get enough of him, wanting him inside but also yearning for his hands on her body, his lips upon hers, his tongue melding with her own.

Her hands raced up and down his back, clutching, squeezing, as she raised her buttocks from the furry rug to meet his every thrust.

He began to move harder. She was bouncing off the floor, struggling to hold back the cries of delight bubbling in her throat for fear of waking Brian.

And then she felt climax coming and feared she would scream despite all resolve. She burrowed her face in his shoulder and held tight, moving fast, fast, faster. Her breath came in steady, ragged gasps.

He pumped harder, and she held on, and then it happened—an explosion of pleasure nonpareil. She started to cry out, and he quickly covered her mouth with his to muffle the sound.

Then his own zenith came, and he seemed to convulse from head to toe as the shudders of release took control of his body.

For long, long moments they lay there, too enraptured from the wonder of it all to either move or speak.

Finally Jackie forced herself to wriggle from beneath

him and stand. "Brian might wake up," she said by way of apology for bringing them back to the real world. "He's in a strange place, you know."

"Not really," Sam said, still on his stomach, face toward the fire. "He stayed here with me a few times before Donna took off."

"But that was a long time ago." She went into the kitchen and gathered her clothes that were on the floor.

Her head was swimming. What was she supposed to do now? She'd never been to bed with anybody but Kevin till now. And they hadn't made love until after they were engaged. So what came next? Did she make more coffee? Did they talk about it? What, exactly, was she supposed to do? Wondering was making her nervous, and she wished it weren't snowing outside, wished it weren't night, and he could leave to end the misery of not knowing what to do, and—

"It was wonderful, Jackie."

His hands were caressing her shoulders as he nuzzled the back of her neck, sending fresh tingles of desire up and down her spine.

What is wrong with you? her mind screamed. She had just had the best sex of her life, and all he had to do was kiss the back of her neck and she was ready to go again.

"Yes, it was," she managed to say, afraid her voice would crack.

Then he spun her around in his arms. "Jackie, I hope you aren't sorry. I mean, I don't want you thinking I intended to seduce you. It just happened, and I hope you don't regret it."

"I...I don't," she said chokily, reveling in the feel of being pressed against him once more. They were still naked, their bodies perspiration-slick.

His kiss was deep, and by the time he let her go, the fires were raging once again.

"I think..." she whispered huskily, "the faux fur is going to get a workout tonight."

Sam lay very still, his head propped on an elbow as he watched her sleeping.

He had been awake since the first light of dawn, which always seemed brighter when the world was buried under snow.

He knew he needed to get going, before anyone was up and about. It wouldn't do to start gossip about him sleeping over with her. Folks wouldn't stop to reason that he'd gotten trapped there during the storm and maybe nothing happened between them, after all. There was too much boredom this time of year, and everyone was hungry for something new to talk about.

But he liked looking at her and hated to leave. She was, beyond a doubt, one hell of a woman. He also knew he'd never enjoyed one more. But that was as far as it was going to go, because he'd be damned if he was going to make a fool of himself again.

Maybe she would wind up staying. If so, then perhaps things might get serious. But he was taking no chances, because he had too much at stake. His son. His farm. And his pride.

He got up slowly, quietly. She stirred, and he covered her with the afghan. The cabin was warm. She'd be fine. So would Brian.

He dressed and left quietly.

Jackie awoke with a start.

There was a noise.

The door closing?

She sat up groggily, wondering why she was on the floor, naked, with an afghan wrapped around her.

And then it all came rushing back.

She scrambled to her feet and ran to the window to look outside. It had stopped snowing, but as best she could guess there was at least four feet on the ground. Worse were the drifts which were much, much deeper.

There were traces where Sam had struggled to get off the porch and go around back to find the snowshoes.

Then she saw him, coming around the side of the cabin, walking in stride, ski poles to help him along.

She watched till he was out of sight, the memories of their lovemaking as warm and glowing as the fire in the grate.

It seemed now like a dream, but she had only to touch her kiss-swollen lips and feel the soreness from their passion in delicate places to know that it was very real indeed.

But, once again, she asked herself, What to do now?

Was it the beginning of something between them or was it to be a one-night stand, brought about by fickle fate and nature's folly?

Only time would tell, and in that instant she realized she didn't have any to spare. Brian would wake up any minute, and she could not let him find her naked.

She scrambled for her clothes just in time, because no sooner had she pulled her shirt over her head than the bedroom door opened and he came padding out sleepily.

She hugged him and told him his daddy would be back soon, that he had gone to get his truck out.

He ate the hot oatmeal she cooked for him with gusto, but when she set the mug of hot chocolate in front of him, smothered in melting marshmallows, she thrilled to see him smile for the first time since she'd known him.

The morning passed slowly. She read to him from a children's book she'd bought from Willa's bookstore. She could not tell whether he enjoyed it, but as least he sat still and listened.

Then, finally, she heard it—the sound of a tractor grinding through the snow.

"Hear that, Brian?" she grabbed his hand and pulled him from the sofa. They went to the door, and she yanked it open. "See? There's your daddy now. He's come to get you."

Sam waved. He was so bundled up she wondered how he could even lift his arm. It was freezing cold, despite the sun, and the snow didn't look as though it had begun to melt at all.

"Everybody okay?" he asked when he drew the tractor right up to the porch steps.

She searched his face for...what? A lusty smile? A knowing smirk? But there was nothing except anticipation for an answer to his question.

It was—she was stunned to realize—as though nothing had happened between them.

"We're fine." She managed to speak as normally as always. "How about your truck?"

"It will take some digging to get it out. I just wanted to come over and get Brian. He's been pestering you long enough. Bonnie wasn't there, so she doesn't know I was out all night."

Translated, she knew, he meant that he did not intend for Bonnie to find out, either.

Well, Jackie wasn't about to climb up on the roof and shout for all the world to hear, either.

He came inside long enough to help get Brian wrapped good and warm, then took him back outside and hoisted him up on the tractor.

"I've got to check around and see if anybody needs anything," he said. "I've got the only tractor around here. You stay warm, and I'll be by later to see how you're doing."

There was meaning there. She sensed it. Felt it. In his voice. In his eyes. And in his soul-warming smile as he nodded goodbye.

He would be back.

Something told her they would make love again. Beyond that, she had no clue.

And, for the time being, perhaps that was best.

Chapter Twelve

The first thing Jackie did when the roads were clear was drive into town to the closest service station and use the pay phone to call Mr. Burkhalter.

When he came on the line, she got right to the point. "How soon before I'll get any money?"

He told her he wasn't sure. "I'll have to check Libby's file and see about when she received hers every year. Hold on."

Jackie tapped her foot impatiently and glanced around to see what was going on in town. The station was on one of the busiest corners, and she could see Main Street. Christmas decorations were everywhere, and workers were busy stringing additional tinsel around the utility poles.

Snow had been scraped from the streets into ugly, dirty piles that would melt slowly. Temperatures had

warmed a bit, and people had to pick their way around
the mud puddles.

The phone was inside the station, and as she waited
for Mr. Burkhalter to return, one of the attendants
walked by and asked, "Is that your car out there, lady?"

She said it was.

He chuckled. "You aren't from around here, are
you?"

"What do you mean?"

"It's not a four-wheel-drive."

He kept on going, whistling as he went. She felt like
yelling after him that the reason she was on the phone
was to try and find a way to get the money to buy one.

Mr. Burkhalter came back on the line. "Looks like
around the first of March. Colton Farms is incorporated,
and corporate returns are due March 15. The accountant
waited till all the tax work was done before paying. Apparently that worked for Libby."

"Libby didn't need the money to buy a car to get
around on these roads. I do, but I'm nearly broke. I don't
have a pay check coming in, you know, and I've spent
almost all my savings on settling in."

"Well, I can always call the accountant for you and
ask him if he can get a partial payment to you right after
the first of the year."

"No, don't do that." If he did, the accountant would
turn around and tell Sam, and she didn't want him to
know any more about her personal business than could
be helped.

Especially after that night.

"I wish there was something I could do. You don't
have any family, do you?"

"No, but it's all right. I'll survive." She hoped. Now
that she and Sam had been intimate, she was all the more

determined to be independent. Otherwise, he might think she was taking advantage of the situation, using him or, worse yet, playing the role of helpless female to get closer to him.

God forbid he think that.

"There's something else," Mr. Burkhalter said. "I was going to write you a letter, but since I have you on the phone I'll just tell you about it. In going over Libby's papers, I discovered that she never had a contract with the Coltons for them to farm her land."

"And what does that mean?"

He laughed. "That Libby, may she rest in peace, did not have any business sense. She let them do whatever they wanted with her land and never asked questions. I suggest that you let me put you in touch with a lawyer in your area, once the will has been probated. He can draw up a contract so everything will be legal, with no misunderstandings."

She wondered how Sam would react to that. "I suppose you're right, but I'm in no hurry. Meanwhile, as soon as I can get some money out of the estate, I'll be grateful."

She thanked him and hung up. She had no idea what she was going to do. Maybe she should not have been so cocky as to think she could survive on her meager savings. Now she needed a job to tide her over, but how could she get to work? Certainly not in the klunker, when she was slipping and sliding all over the roads. It wasn't safe. And certainly not reliable. She had also found out that the nearest nursing home was in Boone. So it was out of the question to look for a job there till she got a car safe for the mountains.

It had been five days since the snow. Sam had been by a couple of times to see if she needed anything, but

Hank had always been with him. For her part, she had avoided eye contact, afraid her feelings might show, because, since that night, she could not get Sam out of her mind.

She told herself it had only happened because of the storm. Soft lights, a glowing fire, music and wine…all had combined to set the stage for passion. She supposed it had to have happened.

So she would not start thinking romance. Jackie cynically mused how Sam might just be trying to get on her good side so he could eventually persuade her to sell and leave. Sure, he had chopped her firewood and done a couple of favors, and he also made sure she was okay during the time she was snowed in, but he might also be gloating inside that she was getting a good dose of what life would be like during the winter.

But she had to put all of it out of her mind in lieu of her first priority, which was finding the means to buy a car.

She had been sipping a Coke she'd gotten from a machine and walked over to toss the can into the trash.

The man who had spoken to her earlier was seated behind a chipped wood desk covered with dirty, oil-stained invoices. Paper cups half-full of coffee, some with cigarette butts floating on top, were crowded into the mess.

She started to walk by but stopped when he said, "I heard you on the phone. When you get the money, I know where you can get a good four-wheel pickup cheap. My brother-in-law is trying to sell it, so you just let me know. The name's Linwood Bean." He tipped his oil-stained cap.

It annoyed her to know he had been listening, but the

phone was just around the corner. Maybe he couldn't help it. She'd give him the benefit of the doubt, anyway.

"Thanks, but I won't be buying anytime soon."

She went her way, thinking how good it felt to be out of the cabin. She was in no hurry to return. Neither was she anxious to get on the road again. The drive in had been tricky. She'd had to constantly be on guard, lest the car slide in mud and send her into a drift of snow left by Sam's tractor when he ploughed.

It was not quite noon, so the café wasn't crowded with the lunch bunch. She enjoyed a cup of chili with melted cheese and sourdough rolls. By the time she finished, the booths were filled and there were customers waiting, so she didn't linger over a second cup of coffee as she would have liked.

Back on the street, she saw the holiday display at the Book Nook and paused for a closer look. Tiny animated elves, dressed in green velvet, sat nodding their heads with interest before a jolly Santa Claus supposedly reading them "The Night Before Christmas." Gift books were scattered amidst artificial snowflakes and glitter.

There were a lot of children's books, and she decided to buy more for Brian for Christmas. He liked it when she read to him, but if Sam kept him from seeing her, maybe he would read to him, or Bonnie. But she would try to get ones with lots of pictures for him to look at in case they didn't.

"Well, hello there," Willa said when Jackie came in. "If you had a phone, I'd have called to ask how you made it through the snow and tell you how happy you made some folks with those trees you gave away."

"I'm glad." Jackie headed straight for the coffee bar.

"The Sunday school class had fun making ornaments, too. You know, kids don't do that anymore. We enjoyed making them, and I think the tree, and Christmas, meant more to us that way. How about you?''

''I'm afraid we had an artificial tree and store-bought decorations. Both my parents worked, so they didn't have a lot of time for things like that.'' Jackie sat down by the stove and took off her jacket.

Willa's place was so cozy. A plate of decorated Christmas cookies was on the table, and she helped herself to a couple. Cold weather revved up her appetite.

No other customers were in the store, so Willa joined her. ''Are you going home for the holidays?''

''No. I don't have any family left. My parents are dead.''

Willa put her hand on her shoulder. ''Oh, honey, I'm sorry. Me and my big mouth. I shouldn't have asked.''

''No, it's all right. It happened a long time ago. They drowned in a boating accident. I was twelve. I went to live with my grandmother. She died right after I graduated from high school, but I was married by then, and—'' Her hand flew to her mouth. What was wrong with her, rattling on like that? She was always a private person. Was that what living alone did—make a person so crazy for company they couldn't stop talking when they got around people?

''I didn't mean to talk so much,'' she said, nervously taking another cookie.

''Oh, that's quite all right. I have that effect on folks, I guess, 'cause if this old stove could talk, it would give away most of the secrets in this town. And don't you worry about being alone for Christmas. I always cook a big turkey and have lots of company. You're invited.''

''I couldn't impose.''

''You won't. Besides, Sam and little Brian are going to be here.''

Jackie shot her a quick glance. Did she know about her and Sam? Of course not. How could she? And what was there to know, anyway? Just because they'd slept together during a snowstorm didn't make them a couple, for gosh sakes. But why had Willa felt the need to mention Sam? Then she told herself she was being silly. Why wouldn't she? After all, it had been the story of the century when it came out she'd come to take over land everyone thought had always belonged to the Colton family.

"You two getting along?" Willa asked, eyes narrowing ever so slightly over the rim of her coffee mug. "Folks figure he wasn't too happy about finding out what his uncle did."

"It was a surprise," Jackie said blandly, as though it were of no real consequence. "And we get along fine. But I don't see him that often," she felt the need to emphasize, "now that the harvest is over."

"Well, you'll see him for Christmas dinner, anyway. He came last year, too. There's always lots of children, and he likes Brian to be around them, though he doesn't play or anything. Just sits there and looks at them." Willa shook her head and made tsking sounds of sympathy. "He's a pitiful little thing. His mother should be horsewhipped for leaving him. What Sam needs to do is find himself a wife. I've been trying to get him interested in my niece, Rosemary. She's from Blowing Rock. A schoolteacher. She was born in the mountains, and he'd never have to worry about her leaving him for the big-city life. She'll be here for Christmas, and you'll meet her."

Jackie primly nibbled at a cookie, figuring if she were eating, her feelings would not show on her face—feelings she told herself she was crazy to be having…like jealousy. "How does Sam feel about that?" She managed to sound nonchalant, as though merely making conversation.

"Well, they've met before, and he knows she's coming," Willa said. "And I mention her to him every time I see him. He said he'd be here, too, so he must be interested."

Jackie felt her heart slide down to her feet. Why wouldn't he be? Willa's niece was mountain born and bred. She was a schoolteacher, which meant she was educated. She would make a good mother for Brian.

And it was, she firmly, furiously, told herself, none of her business. A one-night stand during a snowstorm did not give her any claim on him, and it was best to forget it, as he had obviously done. Every night she had sat by the fire, hoping against hope she'd hear him knock on the door.

Fool, she fiercely chided herself. Jackie Lundigan, you are a fool.

"Are you all right, dear?"

Jackie gave herself a mental shake, returning to the present to see that Willa was watching her with concern.

"I'm fine. Too many cookies, I guess. I probably need to be thinking about getting home. I only stopped in to look over your children's books. I thought I'd get a Christmas present for Brian."

"Oh, that would be nice," Willa said approvingly. "I thought about doing the same, but children can't have too many books, can they? But don't leave just yet. You have to stay for the parade."

"What parade?"

"Didn't Sam tell you?"

Jackie shook her head, clueless.

"Well, it's not really a parade, I guess," Willa said.

"It's just something Sam does every year, and the high school band helps out by leading the way, and—"

The bell over the door jingled. Willa recognized the customer and said, "You'll have to excuse me. That's Pearl Dillinger. I order big-print books for her to read. Her eyes are so bad, even with glasses. Her order came in, and I've got to get it for her. You go and browse in the children's section."

She paused to shake a finger and playfully warn, "I mean it now. Don't you dare go home till after that parade. It's really something to see. It'll get you in the Christmas spirit, for sure."

Jackie had planned to be home well before dark, but her curiosity was piqued. She would have to stay.

She bought two books for Brian. Willa wasn't busy when she rang up the sale so she offered to gift wrap her purchases. Jackie was glad, because she had no paper or bows at home. These would be the only presents she would buy, anyway.

"I really need to get back," she said as Willa cut holiday paper from a big roll. "Why don't you just tell me what's supposed to take place?"

Willa said it would not be the same. "You just have to see it for yourself. Besides, it won't be much longer. See those kids gathering outside?" She nodded toward the front windows.

Jackie turned to see children lining up on the curb. "It must be quite a parade."

"No, nothing like that, but everybody enjoys it."

"What exactly does he do? Dress up like Santa and pass out candy?" That didn't sound like Sam, but she couldn't think of anything else.

"Oh, he does much more than that. And he's been doing it since Brian was about a year old. Between you and me—'' she leaned to whisper, even though no one else was in the store ''—I think he does it because he just plain loves kids and couldn't have the big family he always wanted 'cause Donna was such a little snit. Joan—that's Sam's mother—told me Donna came right out and said she'd never have another baby. She didn't like being pregnant with Brian…said she was miserable the whole time. Joan said it really upset Sam.''

Jackie could understand that but figured it best not to comment.

''So that's why he has the parade,'' Willa said. ''He likes children.''

Jackie wondered why Sam hadn't said anything, but then, why should he? She was not an integral part of his life—except during a snowstorm, she thought wryly.

By the time Willa finished wrapping Brian's presents, people had begun piling into the store with their children, to stay warm till the parade started. Willa reveled in the crowd, and Jackie knew she'd been expecting it when she went into the back and came out with more Christmas cookies and then a big bowl of punch.

To pass the time Jackie went to the hardware store and bought a lock for her front door. And because he was not busy, Tom Haskins explained to her how to install it.

She also bought a drill and screw driver and was taking everything to her car when she heard the distant sound of snare drums.

The sidewalks were crowded, and she was surprised to see so many people. And as the high school band rounded the corner, a cheer went up.

They had tinsel draped around their plumed hats. The majorettes were wearing red velvet outfits. Bright green pompons bounced from their boots when they went into a high stepping routine as the band began to play "Here Comes Santa Claus."

All around her, people were singing along, and she found herself doing the same.

The sun had set, and though it was not quite dark, the town's Christmas lights suddenly came on, and the world around her was a magical place.

Strangely, amidst the joy and revelry going on around her, Jackie felt a part of it all...part of the town, the people and, maybe most important, a sense of the true meaning of Christmas for the first time in her life.

Then the crowd cheered even louder.

Jackie stood on tiptoe, straining to see over the heads of the people in front of her.

"There he is," yelled a little boy, perched on his father's shoulders, waving his arm in a frenzy. "I see him, Daddy. Here he comes."

Despite the noise, Jackie could hear bells making a ching-ching-ching sound. Then she smiled to realize they were sleigh bells, and when the man in front stepped to one side she could see the sleigh. It was real and it was old-fashioned, straight out of a Christmas card. The horses pulling it were wearing harnesses entwined with red ribbons and golden jingling bells.

And then she saw Sam.

He was holding the reins, and the sleigh was loaded down with packages and toys. Behind him, Hank was at the wheel of his truck, the back filled with trees.

Sam reined to a stop. Some of the children began to surge forward. He handed each a gift. Some of the parents went to the truck to lift out a tree.

All the while the band kept playing one Christmas song after another.

A woman standing next to Jackie leaned close to marvel. "Isn't Mr. Colton wonderful? This always puts everyone in the true Christmas spirit."

"He does this every year?" Jackie asked, astonished.

"Oh, yes. He has a gift for every child. Oh, nothing expensive, of course. Just a little something to brighten their day. The trees are to help out families who may have had some financial problems during the year. Afterwards, there's a little party at the National Guard Armory. Some of the churches pitch in to provide refreshments. It's really a nice gathering."

Jackie was deeply touched by it all, for it was a side to Sam she had not known existed.

"I wonder..." she said, more to herself than to the woman, "why he doesn't dress up like Santa."

"Oh, I can't see him doing that," she said. "I mean, the way I hear it, he never intended for it to turn into a parade. He just wanted to do something nice for everybody, and then it sort of mushroomed after that. Isn't it wonderful?"

Yes, Jackie told her, it was.

And so was he.

When the gifts were all given out, and the crowd thinned to head for the armory and the party there, Jackie made her way back to the Book Nook.

"What did I tell you?" Willa greeted effusively. "Wasn't that nice? Didn't it get you in the Christmas spirit?"

"That it did," Jackie agreed with all sincerity. "And it surprised me. I didn't have any idea Sam did something like that."

"Well, he's just modest," Willa said.

Not when he's wearing only an afghan, Jackie secretly, wickedly, thought.

"And he's perfect for Rosemary," Willa said proudly. "They're going to make the perfect match. He's modest, and she's shy."

Jackie ground her teeth together to keep from making a face.

"You'll meet her Christmas," Willa reminded. "And you'll like her."

Jackie managed to keep sarcasm from her tone as she murmured, "I can't wait."

It was very dark when Jackie finally went to her car. She dreaded the drive home, but it was her own fault. She should not have stayed in town. Now she had to pay the price for hanging around to find out about Sam and his parade.

Willa had invited her to stay for supper, but Jackie would not have stayed even if she hadn't wanted to get home before it got any later; if she heard one more word about how wonderful Rosemary was, she was afraid she'd scream.

Crossing the street, she came to an abrupt halt to see Sam leaning against her car.

"What…what are you doing here?" she asked, a thrill rushing through her.

He straightened, pounding his gloved hands together, and gave a huge, mock shiver. "Freezing to death waiting for you to quit gabbing with Willa Kearney."

Stunned, she asked, "You knew where I was?"

"Oh, yeah. I could see you through the windows."

"Well, if you wanted to talk to me, why didn't you come inside instead of standing out here in the cold?"

His laugh was as soft as the Christmas lights reflected in his blue eyes. "You mean you have to ask? Willa is a sweet old soul, but it's hard as heck to get away from her.''

Jackie had to laugh, too, because she had spent the last half hour trying to do just that. "I get your point. So what do you want with me?" She unlocked the door, anything to keep moving so she wouldn't have to look at him, afraid he might see the longing that was surely in her eyes.

"I saw your car parked here and figured you didn't have any business driving home without somebody right behind to make sure you get there okay."

"That...that was nice of you," she managed to say, then added, "and it was also nice what you did today. It must cost you a lot of money."

"Not really. The gifts aren't expensive, but the kids don't care. And I enjoy doing it. But hey, you didn't go to the party."

"No, I went back to Willa's."

There was an awkward silence, then Sam said, "Well, I guess we better be heading home. Bonnie is keeping Brian, and she's probably ready to call it a day."

"You didn't let him come to the parade?"

She saw how the muscle in his jaw tensed. "I didn't figure he'd want to."

He turned and went to his truck, which was parked a few spaces away. She supposed Hank had taken the horses and sleigh back to where they came from and driven his own truck home. She didn't know. She didn't care. All she knew was that Sam cared enough to see her home safely, and that meant more than he could know.

He had stayed far enough behind her that his headlights would not strike her rearview mirror and blind her.

She was surprised when he did not stop at the end of her driveway and back out to go on home. Instead, he drove in right behind her and leaped out of his truck to open her car door for her.

"You might fall in the snow," he said, shining his flashlight to show the way. "I meant to get over here and shovel a path for you to the porch but just haven't gotten around to it. A few people needed me to clear a driveway, since I'm the only one with a blade on my tractor."

He was talking fast and seemed nervous. Jackie sought to put him at ease lest he think she expected him to come inside for a repeat of the other night.

They had reached her door, and she said, "It's nice of you to help so many people, Sam, and I really appreciate your following me home. I'd invite you in for hot chocolate to say thanks, but I know Bonnie is waiting."

"Yeah, I guess she is." He stared down at the toes of his boots.

Jackie opened the door. It was too cold to keep standing there, and she supposed he was determined to make sure she actually got inside the cabin before leaving.

"Well, good night," she said quietly. "And thanks again."

"You're more than welcome."

He turned to go but hesitated, then whirled about. "Jackie, listen, there's something I want to say to you, but I'm afraid you might take it wrong."

She tensed. "Go on."

"It's about what happened the other night."

She had sensed that it was.

"I don't want you to think I meant for it to happen. I did not—" he said firmly "—intend to make love to you. It just happened."

"You sort of already made that clear." A lump had risen in her throat. What he was actually trying to say was that it had been an impulsive act and that she shouldn't expect it to mean anything, because it didn't.

Neither spoke for a moment. Sam kept looking at his boots, and Jackie stared down at hers, as well.

Finally she mustered a smile, although she felt like crying, and said, "Well, let's just forget it, okay? That way it won't be awkward for us to work together."

"Fine." He sounded relieved.

"Then good night. Be careful driving home."

"I will."

He waved without looking at her and made his way back to his truck.

Jackie went inside. She didn't look back, afraid she would burst into tears if she did.

If not for the snow it never would have happened. And now it never would again.

A part of her told her she should be glad, that Sam was so embittered he'd be a long time marrying again, if ever, and certainly not a city girl.

But another part of her ached for what might have been...and sadly, would never be.

Chapter Thirteen

Jackie did not want to go to Willa Kearney's for Christmas dinner, but it seemed the only chance she would have to give Brian his present.

She also had to secretly admit to a small case of cabin fever. The weather had been terrible. Temperatures had warmed, and the rains came, leaving the roads a muddy, mucky mess. There was no telling when the phone company would be able to start running her line.

She did not dare try to take her car out. Hank stopped by every few days to see if she needed anything, and she suspected Sam had told him to because Sam didn't want to come. So, when Hank came Christmas Eve, she asked him if he would give her a ride into town so she could accept Willa's invitation. He said he'd be glad to, then gave her a present Bonnie had made for her—a beautiful hand-knit scarf. Jackie was glad she'd found the time in the past weeks to embroider a pillow and could give that to Bonnie in return.

While she was wrapping it, Hank accepted her offer to have coffee and sat down at the table to watch.

"Seems like we don't have much time to talk anymore," he said. "I'm always in a hurry. You still liking it here?"

"Yes, I sure do. Fact is, I love it." She wasn't about to say she didn't think she would ever get used to such bitter cold weather. She was not going to complain about anything, knowing he would run straight to Sam and tell him.

Hank seemed to read her mind. "You know the boss says you won't stay."

"I know. He's told me that several times. I don't pay any attention to him. You shouldn't, either. I'm here for good."

"You don't get lonesome out here by yourself?"

Actually, that was her biggest problem, but only since she had met Sam. Falling for him had put a kink in her plans for a life of peace and tranquility.

"Of course not," she glibly lied. "I have my books, and I make a stab at writing poetry. I'm also learning to embroider…like this pillow."

"Oh, that's real pretty…real good." His head bobbed up and down.

She had already put Christmas paper around it and doubted he had even noticed what the pillow looked like.

She had been doing some hard thinking lately about the possibility that Sam just might be attracted to Willa's niece. If he married Rosemary, Jackie felt it would be best if she distanced herself. That meant getting serious about taking over her half of the farm, but she still had much to learn, much to do.

She decided to take advantage of the time with Hank and asked, "Do you think that old hothouse out back could be fixed up and put to use?"

"Maybe. The last time anything was planted there was before Sam's daddy died. He had high hopes then for blue spruce, so he started some seedlings there. In fact, he started the ones that Sam cut down to open up your road. But after he died, Sam moved everything to his place."

"Does the heater still work?"

"I reckon. But it's not much. Never was. How come you're asking? Sam's hothouse is big enough."

"I'm thinking about starting some seedlings of my own. Will you help me when you can?"

Hank looked doubtful. "I don't know. It seems a waste of time. Sam's got enough seedlings. Besides, that roof is in bad shape. The heavy snows we've been getting this year isn't making it any better. Sooner or later it's liable to cave in."

"But it will last awhile longer, and next summer I can have a new roof built." She reached across the table to clasp his hand. "What do you say, Hank? Will you help me? All I need is for you to tell me the quantity of seeds I need and how to care for them once they sprout."

With a deep frown he reminded her, "You're going to have to care for them two years before you can put 'em in the field."

"I know that."

"Sam don't think you'll be here that long."

Her sigh was deep and exasperated. "Hank, I don't care what Sam thinks. According to him, I should have already been gone. Now, will you help me or not?"

With absolutely no enthusiasm he said, "All right. I'll tell you what to order, and I'll give you tips along. But that's it. I work for Sam. Not you. And I don't want to get caught in the middle if you two start feuding.''

Jackie felt like telling him if he worked for Sam he also worked for her but knew he would never see it that way. Besides, he might get mad, and she was not about to do anything to alienate him when she had his promise to help.

And she also needed a ride to Willa's.

Jackie was amazed to see where Willa lived behind her store. It was much larger than she had imagined.

She also had it attractively decorated for the holidays. One of Sam's nicer Frasers—or perhaps she should say one of hers and Sam's—dominated the living area. It looked as bright and fresh as the day it had been cut, and its wonderful scent mingled with the delicious aroma of turkey roasting in the oven.

Jackie found herself surrounded by strangers who all seemed to be relatives of Willa. And as she'd said, there were lots of children, all ages and sizes, running around playing with their new toys and making lots of noise.

Willa had to yell above the din to introduce Jackie around.

Jackie had never been good at remembering names and they all seemed to run together. Then Willa said "Rosemary," and she snapped to attention.

"Rosemary is my sister's only daughter," Willa said proudly, giving the tall, shapely young woman a hug, then introducing her to Jackie.

She was anything but what Jackie had expected, which was a rugged mountain woman with strong muscles wearing a flannel shirt, jeans and brogans. There were plenty of those about, because she saw them when she came into town. They lived way up in the most remote part of the mountains and were as hearty as the meals they probably cooked three times a day.

But the svelte woman Jackie found herself shaking hands with did not look as though she ever ate, much less cooked. She was model thin, with long brown hair framing a face that looked as though it had been crafted by a professional makeup artist. She even had a little mole next to her mouth à la Cindy Crawford. And her dress was stunning. Silk the color of holly, it was a simple design that clung to her every curve, spaghetti straps holding the bodice that was molded over perfect breasts.

She had no mountain twang or Southern drawl when she said, "My aunt has told me so much about you, Jackie. I'm very pleased to meet you. And it was so sweet of you to donate all those trees for the poor. It made me think of Sam and the little parade he does every year."

She spoke his name like a caress, her bronze-shaded eyes glancing about the room as she did, obviously looking for him.

Jackie swallowed a groan.

Willa was right.

Rosemary was perfect for Sam. In fact, she was perfect for any man, which prompted her to impishly ask, "Is your husband here?"

Rosemary blinked incredibly long lashes. "No. As a matter of fact, I'm no longer married."

"What happened?" Jackie decided what the heck? She didn't care if Rosemary thought she was nosy. She wanted to find out all she could about the woman who was going to snatch up Sam before she even had a chance to convince him flatlanders weren't so bad when you got to know them.

Rosemary swept her with a cool gaze. "He wanted to

move to Charlotte when he was offered what he considered a job he couldn't turn down. I told him I'd never leave the mountains. He left. I stayed." She shrugged. "No problem.

"Ah, there's Santa Claus," she suddenly cried, dismissing Jackie as though she'd never been there, to move to the door and greet Sam.

"I heard about the parade," she cooed, kissing his cheek. "You are so wonderful to do it every year, Sam."

She knelt to give Brian a hug, and Jackie was envious because her knees didn't pop when they bent like hers always did. Oh, well. She probably had a personal trainer.

She moved on into the kitchen to help get the food on the table. The sooner dinner was over, the sooner she could escape, because something told her Rosemary coming on to Sam was going to be ad nauseum in the worst way.

Sam was seated at the other end of the table, so Jackie was spared having to watch. But she did see a silly smile on his face, like he was enjoying Rosemary's attention.

Later, after pumpkin pie and ambrosia, Jackie found Brian by himself and gave him his gifts. At first, he did not want to open them, but after a little coaxing, he tore off the paper.

When he saw the books, Jackie would have sworn his eyes shone, if only for a second. Then the lackluster look was back, and she wondered if he was thinking how she wouldn't be the one to read them to him, since he had strict orders to stay away from the cabin.

"Don't worry," Jackie whispered in his ear. "I'll find a way to see you, Brian. And sooner or later, when your daddy realizes I'm not going to leave, he won't mind."

But Rosemary might, she mused, because something

told her once Rosemary had her acrylic nails in Sam, she would run the show.

Brian took the books and retreated to a far corner, where he squatted on the floor and leafed through to look at the pictures.

Jackie wished she could leave. The table had been cleared. Now it was time for everyone to catch up on news of the family during the past year. She wasn't family and felt out of place and longed to go, but there was only one problem. It was only four o'clock and Hank had said he couldn't get back to pick her up till after six. He and Bonnie were driving over to Boone to visit her family. So there was nothing for her to do except find somewhere to sit and wait it out.

No one noticed when she slipped through the door into the bookstore. She found it hard to see, because the sky outside was overcast with thick, dark clouds. But she did not turn on a light, because it was so cozy to just sit down on one of the cushioned rockers near the warm woodstove and let her thoughts carry her away.

Why, oh, why, her heart cried, had she let herself get even remotely involved with Sam Colton romantically? Far easier it would have been to despise him. But no. She had to play psychiatrist and conclude that his arrogance and irritability stemmed from what his wife had done. By so doing, she had been able to accept his faults, deal with them. And somewhere along the line, he'd come out of his shell to display that warm, wonderful side that had made her fall like a meteorite to earth. Her landing, of course, had been with about as much of a jolt, because he obviously did not feel the same. He'd just had nothing else to do on a snowy night.

Ah, but that was not fair, she argued with herself. It

had been beautiful—all night long. Certainly not something done in a heated rush to get it over with.

But to think anything could come of their relationship was an exercise in futility, she supposed. He would doubtless want to marry one of his own kind the next time around, someone with roots as deep as his own in his precious mountains. Rosemary fitted the bill, all right, and now Jackie found herself wishing she had stayed home, even if it meant being alone on Christmas day, rather than watch the budding romance unfold right before her eyes.

It had grown darker. Surely it was near six o'clock. She started to get up.

"Don't let me run you off."

She stumbled, nearly fell and sank back into the rocker to grip the arms.

"How...how long have you been here?" she managed to ask as Sam stepped from deep shadows into what light was left.

"A few minutes. You were obviously in another world, because you didn't notice. So I just waited to see how long before you came alive." He walked over to sit down in the rocker next to her. "Christmas make you homesick?"

"No. It's good to be out of the cabin for a little while...even though I love it," she hastened to add, not about to let him think she was unhappy.

"I'm not talking about the cabin. I mean your family. How come you didn't go visit some of them? I told you nothing would be going on around the farm till after the holidays."

"Didn't I tell you? I don't have any family."

"Nobody?"

"Nobody," she confirmed.

He didn't say anything for a few moments, then, "Well, I didn't know you were coming today. It was a surprise seeing you, because I didn't notice your car outside."

She explained about riding with Hank. "He's supposed to pick me up at six. He should be here anytime."

"Don't count on it," he laughed. "You don't know Bonnie when she gets around that clan of hers. They might not be back till midnight."

"Oh, please don't tell me that."

"It's all right. I can take you when I leave, which probably won't be long. Hank knew I was coming, so he'll figure you got a ride with me, anyway."

"Why are you leaving so early?"

"I just feel a little out of place. I'm not one of Willa's relatives. She treats me like I am, though, so I shouldn't complain."

Jackie could not resist teasing, "But if she gets her way, you will be a relative."

"What's that supposed to mean?"

"In a word—Rosemary."

Amused, he asked, "Is it that obvious?"

"Well, I don't know about other people, but Willa told me beforehand that she hoped you two got together. She's really pretty," Jackie added, trying to sound complimentary, approving…anything to keep her jealousy from showing.

"You don't know me very well yet, Jackie," he said quietly. "If you did, you'd know she's not my type. Too much like Donna."

"But Donna wasn't from around here. Rosemary is."

"That's not what I'm talking about. Like Donna, Rosemary is more concerned with herself, her needs, than anyone else. I have a friend who knew her husband.

He told me that's why he left her. It's always about her…. Just like Donna," he added thickly, bitterly.

Jackie resisted the impulse to sigh with relief.

"Besides," he continued, "I don't need a wife. I get along just fine without one."

Jackie felt like remarking that Brian certainly didn't get along fine without a mother, but decided to keep her mouth shut. Nothing she said would make any difference, anyway.

Then, as gentle as the whispered touch of a firefly, his hand found hers in the darkness. Squeezing her fingertips, he said, "That doesn't mean I don't need a woman, Jackie. What we shared the other night was really special. I can't stop thinking about it, and I'm afraid I said all the wrong things afterward."

"It doesn't matter." She could barely speak as she fought to keep from trembling. The heat of his nearness was making her insides do crazy things. "It…it just happened, like you said."

"What I said—" he leaned closer, and instead of squeezing her fingers grasped her whole hand tightly "—came out all wrong. I was trying to tell you that I didn't set out to make love to you, but I'm glad I did. The only thing is—I can't offer you anything more, like marriage."

"Well…well…" She was sputtering, feeling like an idiot. She swallowed hard and forced the words past her trembling lips, "I don't expect you to. We just have to forget it and go on as we have been—as business partners and friends."

"I've got lots of women friends, Jackie, but they never make me want to do this…."

His arms went around her, pulling her close. His kiss

was long and deep, and Jackie wished it could last forever.

He drew back ever so slightly, his lips still brushing hers as he whispered, ''We've both had a lot of pain, Jackie, but we can give each other a lot of pleasure. Tell me to go to hell if you will, but I won't apologize for being a man...won't apologize for wanting a woman who makes me crazy—''

''Yoo-hoo. Sam, are you in here?''

They sprang apart just before Rosemary hit a switch to flood the room with light.

She saw them and frowned. ''Well, why are you two sitting here in the dark?''

''It wasn't dark when we sat down,'' Sam said, getting to his feet. ''We just got to talking business, and time slipped away.''

''Oh, that's right.'' Her brow relaxed. ''Aunt Willa said you two farm together. Anyway, sorry to interrupt but it's time for us to go.''

Sam looked confused. ''Us?''

Jackie could only sit there, not trusting her legs to hold her up, because she was still deeply shaken from Sam's kiss. If Rosemary hadn't intruded, she was sure he would have said something about seeing her later. As it was, everything was in limbo with nothing resolved.

''Yes, us, silly,'' Rosemary was saying. She had slipped her arm through his. ''You will be a dear and drive me home, won't you? I rode over with Uncle Billy, but he's had too much spiked eggnog, and he's probably going to spend the night on Aunt Willa's couch.''

Jackie turned her head away so Rosemary wouldn't see her make a face. Why couldn't she sleep over at her aunt Willa's, too?

Rosemary continued, ''She says she'll take Brian

home in the morning. He fell asleep and she put him in her bed, and there's no need to wake him up and take him out in the cold.''

Sam, ever polite and obliging, said, ''Well, okay.'' Then, to Jackie, ''Get your coat and let's go.''

''Where is she going?'' Rosemary coolly asked.

''Home. Like you. I'm giving her a ride. She lives on the farm, too. She's my neighbor.''

Who wants to be your lover, Jackie silently, wickedly thought, starting tonight if you can get rid of the Cindy Crawford wannabe.

Rosemary's lip jutted out in a baby pout. ''Well, I hope you're taking her home first. I made a special dessert for you, and—''

''And I'm more stuffed than the turkey before we lit into him like a pack of vultures.'' He laughed and patted his stomach. ''Really, Rosemary, I can't eat another bite.''

Jackie sprang to her feet. She and Sam had just shared a special moment and maybe sometime soon they would share another. But for the time being, the magic had ended. ''It's okay. You two go ahead. Hank will be along sooner or later, and I can help Willa finish cleaning up.''

She walked on out before Sam could protest, but felt his eyes on her all the while.

Jackie couldn't sleep.

Tossing and turning, she would fling away the blankets only to snatch them up seconds later when she started shivering.

She was torturing herself thinking about what might have happened had Rosemary not ruined it all. Sam would have brought her home and been in no hurry to leave since Brian was taken care of till morning. They would have made sweet, tender love and then talked till dawn. She would have made breakfast, and they'd have talked some more, grown close and it would have been the beginning of a wonderful new relationship.

And then what?

She rolled over on her side.

Was that all she wanted—a relationship based on sex? He said he couldn't offer marriage, and she wasn't sure how she would react if he ever did. Only time would tell, but it looked like Rosemary was going to complicate things.

Suddenly she heard a knock on the front door and sat straight up in bed, jerking the blankets up to her chin. It was the middle of the night.

"Jackie, it's me—Sam."

She bounded out of bed, not bothering to search for her slippers. "What are you doing here at this hour?" She fumbled with the lock she'd installed and opened the door.

A blast of frigid air blew in with him, and he quickly closed the door with his foot. "I couldn't let the evening end like it did, Jackie. It just seems like I never get all the right words out in time."

She had switched on a lamp on her way across the room, and she could see the worry etched in his face. It seemed so natural to reach and soothingly trail her fingertips down his cheek.

"Do we have to talk about it now?" she asked.

"No," he smiled, "we don't."

There was the dimple again, and she stood on tiptoe to press her lips against it.

In one fluid motion, he lifted her in his arms and carried her into the bedroom.

He laid her down on the bed, then began stripping off his clothes, his eyes burning into hers.

Then he was beside her to slowly, gently, raise her gown. His breath caught at the sight of her naked body. "You," he whispered, "are beautiful."

His tongue brushed her lips, coaxing them apart as he tortured her with teasing tenderness. She arched against him, arms going around his neck to bring him closer.

She trailed her hands down his back, loving the feel of his rippling muscles. A heated rush was building, pulsing through her veins to course all through her body.

He rolled to one side, his knee slipping between her legs to spread them apart. Then his hand traveled downward to become a hot sword of pleasure as he began to stroke and massage, then plunge in and upward, thrusting to and fro.

She moaned, arching her neck, her breasts pushing against him as he dipped his mouth to lick each nipple in turn.

She tried to get closer, pushing her hips upon him, feeling his hard shaft hot and pulsating against her. He held back, making her want him all the more.

At last he could stand it no longer and guided her up and onto her knees.

"I want to be deep inside you," he said, clutching her by her waist and positioning himself between her thighs. "I want to hold you tight and give you everything I have to give."

And Jackie wanted it all...so much so that she thought if he didn't take her then and there she would surely die.

He pushed into her, and a cry of delight escaped her lips. Then he was moving, and she felt him deep and hard and reveled in every thrust. He clutched her waist, then her breasts. She matched his rhythm. Then she felt him quicken just as the first pulses of ecstasy began for her.

They peaked together and clung together, for long, tender moments. At last, spent, they tumbled forward to lay spoonlike, with Jackie's back cuddled against him.

She shuddered and felt goose bumps dance up and down her spine as his warm lips pressed against her shoulder.

Jackie knew in that crystallized moment that in her heart she would always want him.

But deep down she knew she would never be content with an endless affair.

It was, for the moment, as good as it gets...as the saying went.

And, heart shuddering, she wondered just how long the goodness would last.

Sam loved watching Jackie as she slept.

The truth was, he loved everything about her, only he had no intentions of letting her know that. If she did stay it had to be by her own volition. He did not want her feelings for him to have any influence on her decision. Well he knew errant choices could be made when passion got in the way of reason. She seemed to be adjusting to the life, but he had to be sure. Not only for his sake...but Brian's, as well.

He knew it seemed hard-hearted, cruel almost, to deny his son the pleasure of being around someone he so obviously adored. But he had to, at all costs, protect him from another hurt.

And maybe, Sam thought as he pressed his lips to her cheek and held her, he wanted to spare himself another heartbreak, as well.

Chapter Fourteen

Jackie found herself living for the times when she could be with Sam, as the weeks slowly drifted by.

New Year's came and went. January passed in a snowy, icy blur with February swirling right behind it as winter vented its fury upon the mountains.

She was able to finally work on the poetry she had longed to for so long. She dabbled with painting. And her stack of unread books grew smaller and smaller.

Sometimes Sam brought Brian with him, and she would whip up something fun for them to eat—spaghetti, sloppy Joes, lasagna. She could also make a terrific pan pizza that Sam loved, which inspired him to say that for the first time he didn't mind not being able to have it delivered.

"When did you ever have it delivered?" she asked, laughing.

He said back in his college days, where fast food was what he'd actually majored in.

Brian still didn't speak. Otherwise, he was a normal little boy. He watched television. He liked to play Nintendo. He enjoyed having someone read to him.

"I have to make a decision very soon," Sam said one evening as they sat on the sofa enjoying spiced tea while Brian sat at the kitchen table putting a puzzle together. "He'll be old enough to start school next fall, but he can't go the way he is now."

Jackie had avoided broaching the subject, but since Sam opened it up, she plunged right in, keeping her voice low so Brian wouldn't hear. "I still don't understand how anyone could say he's retarded. He's very bright."

"And I agree. But my mother doesn't, and she says he's never going to be happy until he's with his own kind."

"And what is his own kind?" Jackie challenged, struggling to keep a rein on her temper. She told herself to tread lightly where Sam's mother was concerned, but it made her furious to hear that Joan Colton could say such a thing.

"Well, I guess we'll find out, if I decide to send him to the place she's found for him."

"And where is that?"

"Over near the coast—Goldsboro."

Jackie had been leaning against him, enjoying the feel of her body close to his, but she sat straight up to cry, "You're talking about O'Berry Center, aren't you? Sam, you can't send him there. I know that place. It's where they put seriously impaired children and adults. It's a wonderful place, true, but Brian doesn't belong there."

"My mother's doctor thinks he does."

Jackie became huffy then, not caring if he resented her criticism of his mother. "Well, Brian is your son. Not hers. And I think it's terrible that a grandmother has no other solution than to shut her grandson away with people who are really badly off."

To her surprise Sam didn't seem to mind her censure. "I agree she's overreacting, but she's changed since Dad died. She's married to a man now who is completely different, and her attitude is that everything can be fixed with money since they seem to have plenty of it. But she's not a bad person, Jackie, believe me," he added quietly, searching her face for some sign that she understood. "And you have to admit he's not getting any better here. It can't go on. It's not fair to him."

"When are they going to put the phone line in?" Jackie suddenly wanted to know.

Surprised by the abrupt change of subject, Sam said it might be in another week. "I talked to one of the linemen in town a couple of days ago. He said the weather is supposed to break soon. We'll get some unseasonably warm weather. They plan to take advantage of it and get out here. Why?"

"Just wondering," she said. She kept her plan to contact some doctors to herself, not wanting to get Sam's hopes up…and also not wanting him annoyed at what he might consider meddling.

He had told her she was being spoiled by the good weather, that she still hadn't experienced the havoc winter could wreak and might be in for a rude awakening one of these days.

Jackie didn't mind. What she did mind, however, was the ambivalence with which Sam seemed to regard the two of them. He was as dynamic as ever in his lovemaking. They were bold, adventuresome, and he showed her ways of pleasure she never knew existed. As for her part, she was always willing to do anything different if it made him happy. But once it was over, it was back to life as normal, and they seemed no more than business partners.

So Jackie began to ask herself if she could be content with lust and a few thousand Christmas trees…because it was starting to seem that was all they would ever have.

Meanwhile, she decided to go ahead with her plans to run operations on her land by herself. She spent the rest of her money on seeds, and Hank helped her plant the beds. She tended them carefully, stoking the old wood stove on freezing-cold nights to keep the vulnerable sprouts warm.

She thought of the two years it would take for the seedlings to be big enough to transplant and couldn't help wondering what her life would be like then. She knew she loved Sam but feared she was just filling a physical need for him and held no place in his heart.

She also knew she was getting stressed out, which was something she had foolishly believed would never happen after she moved to the mountains. Not only did she stay torn over Sam but over Brian, as well. She adored him and it broke her heart to think of him having to leave his home…his father.

As Sam had told her, the weather did turn exceptionally warm by the end of February. Lines were installed, and the very first day she could use her phone, she started making calls.

It took a while to make her way through the list of people she hadn't talked to in ages, in order to get the information she needed. Everyone wanted to know

where she was, and when she told them, they had a
zillion questions.

Though she didn't ask about Kevin whenever she
spoke to mutual friends, she supposed it was only natural
for them to mention him. Three times she had to hear
that he was now the father of a baby girl; she was
pleased that it didn't bother her at all. She didn't even
care enough about him to hold a grudge.

Her phone calls resulted in obtaining the name of Jef-
frey Valcross, a doctor at Duke University who special-
ized in aphasia—the loss of the power of expression by
speech, writing or signs.

She placed several calls to his office before she finally
managed to get him on the line, and then he was in a
hurry. As briefly as possible she told him of Brian's
situation.

"Well, hasn't he been seen by a doctor there?" he
asked impatiently. "I mean, you tell me he hasn't uttered
a word in sixteen months. Surely you've sought treat-
ment there. Have your doctor contact me, and I'll be
glad to set up an appointment for consultation."

She rushed to explain, "You don't understand. He has
been examined by a doctor, and he thinks it's some kind
of stress disorder that he'll eventually get over, but ad-
vises that he be sent to O'Berry."

"That sounds reasonable. If there's no other explanation…"

"But I think there is," she argued. "I think it was
caused by the little boy waking up to see his mother
leaving with another man, and—"

He cut her off with an exasperated sigh and said,
"Then you'd be talking about psychogenic aphasia,
sometimes called shock aphasia. If that's the case, he'd
need extensive therapy. Now, that's all I can tell you

right now, and I do have a busy schedule. If you want to talk more about this, make an appointment. I'm sorry to be so abrupt, and I don't mean to be rude, but I do have to go.''

Jackie was disheartened and discouraged, because she really didn't know any more than she did before making the phone calls. But if Sam would agree to taking Brian to Duke, then maybe Dr. Valcross could help him.

When she mentioned it, though, Sam didn't share her enthusiasm. ''I just can't see dragging him to another doctor to hear the same thing—he needs long-term care. I hate like hell to send him away, but I don't see that I've got any choice.''

She didn't argue. What was the point? Sam was Brian's father. He was the one to make the decisions as to his care.

She was merely the woman he made love to when the notion struck.

And, she was pained to think, that notion did not seem to be striking quite as often.

Was it her imagination, she wondered, or was Sam really pulling away from her? More and more he seemed to be holding back, somehow.

Yet she had to remind herself how he had promised nothing. So she should expect nothing...and had no cause for complaint.

But still she worried, because she loved him.

In early March she received a sizable check for her share of the profits from the Colton tree farm. With it was a contract and a letter from Sam's accountant explaining that he had advised Sam it was only proper that they have an agreement in writing.

She immediately went to the phone and called him to

ask for an explanation and said, "Libby Pratt never had a contract."

Dan Cowley, the accountant, was polite and cordial. "That's true. She never asked for one."

"Whose idea was this?"

"Mine. I thought since you're an active partner it would be best. Sam agreed, so I had my company's attorney draw it up."

She was really becoming indignant. "Funny he didn't mention it to me."

"He thought it best I handle it. Now, of course, you will want to have your attorney go over it, but it just says in writing what has always been understood verbally. You get half the profits after expenses."

She stared at the contract she held in her shaking hand. It all seemed so cold, so formal. But what struck a nerve was how Sam hadn't said a word. He just took it for granted, despite how she'd told him otherwise, that things would go on as they had been. "Well, Mr. Cowley," she said finally, "the fact of the matter is I don't want a contract, either."

He gave a little laugh. "But that's not good business, Ms. Lundigan. It was a sentimental thing with Ms. Pratt, I believe. You see, I knew all about her owning the land. The family had to take me into their confidence because I handle their books, and they knew I'd never tell anybody. But I did advise them, many times, to get something in writing. It's just good business. They didn't listen. Apparently Sam has seen the wisdom. And after all," he added, "it's to your benefit."

"Is it now?" She wondered if Sam had set it up to protect his interest when the day came she went out on her own. They hadn't discussed it, and she had put off telling him till spring, figuring he had enough on his mind with having to make the decision about sending Brian away.

As Dan Cowley talked on, trying to convince her to go along with the contract, she read the rest of the pages she had only glanced at before. Then the clause about the trees on her land leaped out at her.

Sam wanted half of them. The agreement would be that should she, at any time, decide not to renew the contract, then he would receive half of the profit from the sale of the trees growing on her property at that time, in compensation for labor.

"No way," she cried.

Dan Cowley was in the middle of a sentence and cut himself off to ask, "I beg your pardon?"

"This is something Sam should have discussed with me first. I've nothing else to say to you, Mr. Cowley."

She hung up the phone and laughed at the ludicrousness of it all, to keep from bursting into tears.

It was time to have Mr. Burkhalter give her the name of the lawyer he had mentioned the last time they had talked. She was sure she was going to need him when Sam found out she had refused to sign. She might even find herself embroiled in a lawsuit, because he obviously was not going to give up his claim on several thousand trees that he had planted. They might have talked about it before, but never for a minute did she take him seriously. She could not survive on the share she would receive after he took his cut.

And, with fists clenched, she cursed herself for ever having thought all of this would be just one, happy adventure.

She wondered how soon she would hear from Sam, but didn't have long to wait. He phoned within the hour.

Without fanfare, he got right to the point. "Dan says you won't sign the contract."

She bounced right back. "And your point is?"

"I want to know why."

"I don't like some of your terms. I'm going to see my own lawyer."

"What is it you object to, Jackie?" She could tell he was really agitated.

"Well," she began, heart pounding to hear his voice, regardless of the mood he was in, "I want to branch out on my own and start my own farm, beginning now. I know there won't be any profit for a while, but I plan to go back to work."

"Jackie, this doesn't make sense."

It did to her. It was her lifeline to keeping her perspective, when she ultimately had to accept the fact that she was his lover and nothing more. And that meant she had to be able to take care of herself, because she sure as heck couldn't depend on him to do it. Sooner or later the right woman would come along. He'd get married. And then what would she be to him? Nothing but his ex-lover and half owner of the farm. So she had to have independence if she were to survive.

"It makes sense to me," she said finally. "It's how I want it, Sam. It's how it has to be. You and I—" she hesitated, then plunged ahead to say with all candor "—need to keep our personal lives separate from business. I'm afraid we haven't been doing a very good job of that."

"Maybe not, but your going out on your own is poor judgment, Jackie. You won't make it without me and my operation. Besides, regardless of what's between us personally, I can't let you do it."

"You can't stop me. And I read the clause about your

wanting half my trees for the labor of having planted them. Well, what about the ones on yours? Was half the expense of those deducted from Libby's checks and the one I just received? If so, I want half the profit.''

"This," he said icily, "is getting out of hand. And I told Dan not to put that clause in there, but evidently he forgot."

"Or maybe you just forgot to tell him," she snapped.

"Jackie, this is ridiculous."

"Only because you've made it so."

His sigh was loud, long and exaggerated. "Look, we need to talk. I haven't said anything, because I was hoping you were just fooling around, but Hank told me about helping you set up the old hothouse and plant seedlings. I'd seen the smoke coming out of the chimney and, again, didn't say anything, but evidently this is something you've been planning behind my back for a long time, and I'd like to know why."

"Because..." She was floundering. She had kept it from him, but only due to her fear that at any time he would end what was between them. She had wanted something to fall back on if that happened, only she didn't have the nerve to tell him so. Then he would know what her pride would not allow her to tell him— that she had fallen in love with him.

"Oh, hell," she said finally, "I don't know. I guess because when you come right down to it, it wasn't any of your business."

"I think," he said, taking a deep breath and letting it out slowly, "that maybe we should just let the lawyers handle it. I guess we didn't spend enough time talking and never really knew each other at all."

She knew what he meant. The second they were alone, they always jumped into each other's arms and never got around to anything else. But it was wonderful. The best lovemaking Jackie could imagine. And always afterward he would hold her for a long, long time like he couldn't stand to let her go.

But now it seemed they should have spent more time talking and getting to really know each other. They were at odds with each other now, and all because of the land. Maybe it had been a symbol of love to Libby, but to Jackie it was now the opposite, and she found herself close to hating it.

"This isn't getting us anywhere," Jackie said finally. "And I have other business to take care of. Goodbye."

She hung up the phone, grabbed her purse, and drove her old car to town for what would be its last trip—with her at the wheel, anyway.

Two hours later, after depositing her check, she was driving Linwood Bean's cousin's four-wheel-drive pickup truck. He had taken her car in trade, after all, and she thought she'd made a pretty good deal for herself. She could also get to Boone in most any kind of weather, if she ever got a job there. For the time being, she needed to get busy on the farm—her farm—to be ready for spring and all the work that would have to be done then.

But despite being pleased over the truck, Jackie was truly down in the dumps. She had, for all intents and purposes, ended her relationship with Sam in every way. Loving him as she did, that was pretty hard to bear.

She also felt terrible about Brian. She would miss him so much, for she had come to love him, too.

But life had to go on. Somehow she would eventually find a way to mend her aching heart, and she found herself wishing she had not been so hasty to end things. Still, it was probably best that things had come to a head, and maybe Sam felt the same way.

With the break in the weather, Jackie drove to Boone and made the rounds of nursing homes. There were no openings for dieticians, but she filled out applications, anyway. She was told, however, that she could work as a nursing assistant. It was not something she wanted. The hours were long, and the pay wasn't much, but she said she would keep it in mind. When her money ran out she would have no choice.

On her way back from Boone she went to see a woman Tom Haskins had told her about the last time she was in his store. The woman and her husband had a small tree farm, but the husband had recently died. Deciding not to bother growing trees any longer, the woman wanted to sell the seedlings in their hothouse. So she called the hardware and feed stores around to leave word in case anyone was interested in buying them. Some of them would be ready to set in the field in the spring, so Jackie happily bought all of those. It put quite a dent in her checkbook, but it would give her a head start on her own crop of Christmas trees.

Then winter returned with a vengeance. First, due to the warm weather, the rains came in a deluge. And when the temperature took a nosedive as a cold front came roaring in, the rain changed to sleet.

There had been an ice storm in January, and Sam had gone out with Hank to shake the young trees so the weight of the ice would not break tender branches.

As she stood at the window watching the smaller trees crusting with ice, she half expected to see Sam turn in the driveway. It had been over two weeks since she had talked to him, and there had been no contact. But he wouldn't let the trees be damaged just because he was angry with her. Yet, as the hours passed and the ice grew heavier, she began to wonder.

Finally, angrily, she went to the phone and called him. If he didn't want to do anything about it, fine, but he could at least send Hank over, and she would bundle up and work right alongside him.

The woman who answered the phone was not Bonnie. The voice was vaguely familiar, but she couldn't place it as she asked to speak to Sam.

"Oh, he can't come to the phone," the woman cooed. "This is Rosemary. Can I help you?"

"Is Bonnie there?" Jackie asked tightly.

"No. I'm taking care of things around here now. Who is this, anyway?" she asked testily.

"Never mind." Jackie dropped the phone like it was on fire.

No wonder he wasn't out shaking ice off tree limbs, she fumed, as she began pulling on heavy winter gear. He was cuddled up with Rosemary, damn him. And what did she mean—she was taking care of things?

Jackie paced about angrily, then told herself to get her act together. Sure, she cared, and more and more she was asking why if she really wanted to torture herself by being around him even in a remote way.

But first things first. She had to save what trees she could.

By the time she had tramped up and down the seemingly endless rows, shaking each branch free of the killing ice, Jackie felt as if she was the one who was frozen.

Afterward, she hurried to fill the tub with hot water while she stripped off her clothes. She planned to soak to her very bones and then wrap up in blankets, huddle in front of the fire and sip wine till she fell asleep.

Still shivering, she didn't even bother to test the water

but jumped right in with both feet—and promptly jumped right back out again screaming.

It was as cold as the ice she had shaken off the trees. What the heck was going on?

Yanking on her robe, she ran into the kitchen where the hot-water heater was located under a cabinet.

''Oh, no,'' she groaned, seeing the telltale glow of the light that meant it wasn't working. The damn thing had probably frozen during the night. And with ice on the highways, there was no way a plumber was going to come out and fix it before a major thaw.

Slapping her palms against her forehead, she told herself not to panic. The fireplace of course still worked. She had a big pot and would just heat water and pour it into the tub. A bit of work, but so what? She was learning to be self-sufficient, by God, and nothing was going to get her down. At least the power was still on.

And, in that precise moment, it went off, the lights blinking a few times as if in mockery.

But Jackie was not to be outdone. She took out the oil lantern and candles and soon had mellow light to serve her needs.

Nothing was going to lick her. Let Sam Colter veg out with his Cindy Crawford wannabe. She would show him she could get by fine without him. What annoyed her, however, was the thought that the young trees at Sam's place were going to be broken down by the ice. But if he didn't care why should she? They were no longer partners, and she was looking after her interests and to heck with his.

It took a while to heat enough water, but eventually Jackie had her bath. Then she poured herself a glass of wine and flopped on the sofa.

Life, she commanded herself to believe, was

good...or at least it was going to be. All she had to do was hang in there.

She was about to doze off when there was a loud banging on the door.

Groggily she ran to open it and found Hank standing there.

"Sorry I was so late gettin' here to shake your trees, Jackie. I see you've already done it."

He looked upset, and she told him it was all right. "Come on in. You look like you could use some coffee to warm you up."

He continued to stand there, as though he had something to say but didn't know how.

"Hank, what is it?" she prodded, gripping the door for support, because she had a feeling this was not good.

"Have you checked your hothouse lately?"

"Well, yes," she said uncertainly. "When I finished with the trees, I made sure the stove was full of wood and working okay."

"That's not what I mean," he said, eyes filled with pity. "Jackie, I hate to tell you this, but the roof caved in."

Chapter Fifteen

Jackie was sitting on the front porch, when she had the feeling someone was watching her.

Whipping her head about, she saw it was Brian, peeking around the corner.

She smiled, despite how miserable she was feeling at the moment. So what if it was a gorgeous day, spring bursting forth in all its glory? The rhododendron was loaded with buds, and the mountain laurel was already beginning to bloom. She had seen her first hummingbird, and the apple trees and blackberry bushes were dotted with tiny white flowers which forecast a bumper season.

But none of it meant anything to Jackie, because she felt like a complete failure.

"Come on over here and sit down," she called to Brian, waving. "And I don't care what your daddy says. You can stay as long as you want to."

He didn't hesitate, scampering around the corner to

take the steps two at a time. Eagerly he climbed into the chair beside her, gripped the arms and gave her a heart-melting grin as he began to rock.

''So how are things over your way?'' she asked him, knowing there would be no answer.

She tried not to think about Sam but couldn't help it, not when he owned a piece of her heart. It had been four weeks since the big ice storm had made the roof of her hothouse collapse, destroying all the seedlings. He had not been by to see her. Hank said he hadn't had much to say when he heard about it.

Hank hadn't offered explanation as to Rosemary's presence during the storm, and she hadn't asked him. In a way she wondered, but in another, she didn't want to know. All that mattered—and hurt so very, very badly— was that Sam had apparently wasted no time in getting over her.

She had called Mr. Burkhalter and got the name of the lawyer he wanted her to see. But that was as far as it had gone. She couldn't see going to the expense of having a conference with him, especially when she was so tight on money, due to buying the truck and all of the widow's seedlings. Seedlings, especially good Frasers, as those had been, did not come cheap.

Besides, she'd heard nothing from Sam about it, and the way she saw it, it was his problem. She would make enough from the seven-year-old trees ready to be harvested come fall to keep her going for a while, if he didn't file some sort of lawsuit to claim his share.

Her problem, however, stemmed from wondering whether she wanted to stay. True, she loved the beauty of the mountains, but life had become a turmoil once she let herself so foolishly fall in love with Sam.

Brian continued to happily rock to and fro. She

watched him and wondered when he would be leaving. It was spring. Sam had said he'd make up his mind then. She was sure he would decide to send his son away.

All of a sudden Brian jumped down from the chair and ran inside. Jackie wondered what he was after. He might be using the bathroom, but if he didn't return soon she would have to check on him. She regretted there were no treats to offer him. She just didn't care about baking anymore.

As she waited for Brian, she reread the letter from Madeline Stallings, Dove Haven's director and an old friend.

Madeline went into detail about how displeased everyone was with the dietician that had taken Jackie's place. She had recently given her notice, and Madeline was relieved. Then she went on to ask in a tongue-in-cheek manner if Jackie might have had her fill of mountain living by now and would consider coming back.

She was not, Jackie knew, altogether joking. The job would be hers if she wanted it. The question was—did she?

She looked around at the beauty of her surroundings. If she could just get over Sam, she was sure she could have a good life here. But try as she might, she could not forget him.

Brian came back out, and she saw that he was carrying one of the books she had bought for him.

"So you want me to read to you?" she asked, pleased.

For answer, he surprised her by climbing right up in her lap, something he had never done before.

Settling back, the top of his head tucked under her chin, Jackie wrapped her arms about him and opened the book to read.

And all the while her heart was filled to overflowing

to think how crazy she was about him…and how much she was going to miss him.

The morning passed so quickly. Jackie finished the book, and he ran and got another. Then she found a jar of peanut butter and some bread that wasn't quite stale. She also had a box of cookies, so they wound up with a nice little picnic.

They sat on a blanket by the stream. Brian ate his fill, then lay back, his head in her lap, as they watched big, puffy clouds roll across the bright blue sky. Jackie pointed out different shapes that reminded her of animals.

"See, Brian? That one looks like a poodle dog, doesn't it? And see the other one? It's an old man with a beard. Maybe its your grandfather smiling down from heaven."

His eyes showed more expression than normal, with a little glimmer of interest. She continued to ask him questions, hoping against hope that he would suddenly answer. But he remained silent, and she had begun to fear he always would. She could only pray the doctors would not give up on him, would not accept the theory that he had been mentally unstable all along, and the trauma of his mother leaving just pushed him over the edge.

Finally, Brian fell asleep. Jackie was just about to also doze off when she heard the sound of a car coming up the road.

Easing Brian's head from her lap, she left him where he was and went around the cabin.

The car was not one she had seen before. Neither was it the kind to be driving in the mountains—a long, sleek sedan.

A man was behind the wheel. A woman beside him.

The woman opened her door and got out, and Jackie noticed at once how elegantly she was dressed in a green silk pantsuit, matching heels, her hair upswept in a dramatic bun and accented by huge emerald eardrops.

Her makeup was also done to perfection, and for an instant reminded Jackie of Rosemary.

"Hello, there," she called merrily, walking toward her while the man waited in the car. "You must be Jackie. Willa told me all about you. I'm Joan, Sam's mother."

For an instant, Jackie was so surprised she couldn't find her voice, then managed to say, "I'm pleased to meet you," and held out her hand.

Joan shook it, then stood back to glance around and marvel, "My, you really have fixed this place up. Sam's great-uncle built it, intending to live in it with his bride when he came back from the war, but as you know, he never came back."

Jackie had not known that, but suspected as much. "It's very cozy. I enjoy it."

"Well, welcome to the mountains."

She continued to glance around as though she were looking for something.

Hesitantly, Jackie offered, "Would you like some coffee?"

Joan held up a perfectly manicured hand, the diamond rings on her fingers sparkling in the sun. "No, no. I'm looking for Brian. He sneaked off this morning. Sam said he thought he might be here."

"As a matter of fact, he is," Jackie confirmed. "He's napping by the stream. We had a little picnic, and he fell asleep."

"Oh, that's sweet," Joan said. "I'll go get him, and don't worry—he won't be bothering you much longer.

Tomorrow afternoon when I leave I'll be taking him with me." She gave a little sigh of relief to explain, "Sam has finally agreed it's best, and I am so glad. Heaven only knows how I have worried about that boy."

Jackie bit her lip for silence only for an instant, then, telling herself she had nothing to lose, blurted out, "I don't think that place in Goldsboro is right for Brian. He's not retarded. He's a bright little boy. He loves for me to read to him and tell him things, and I believe he understands everything I say to him. There's nothing wrong with him, except that he can't talk. And I think he's suffering from what's called psychogenic aphasia, and—"

"Are you a child psychologist, Jackie?" Joan interrupted to coolly ask with brows raised.

"No, but—"

"Have you had any training in child psychiatry at all?"

"That's not the point, and—"

Again Joan interrupted to ask, "What exactly is your field?"

"My…my field?" Jackie blinked. "Why, I'm a licensed dietician."

"Then you have no experience with this sort of thing, do you? You don't even have children of your own to know anything at all about them."

By then Jackie was mad and not about to hold back. "No, but it doesn't take a degree in psychiatry to know there's nothing mentally wrong with Brian. And why are you so insistent to lock him away? He's your grandson, for heaven's sake. You ought to want to help him."

Joan's carefully made-up eyes narrowed. "My dear, I know much more about the situation than you. I also know that Brian will not receive the kind of help he needs up here in these mountains. He hasn't spoken a word in almost two years, and he isn't going to unless he has help. Now," she said coldly, "I will take my grandson and leave."

She started to walk past Jackie.

Jackie moved to block her.

"No wonder Sam objected to him coming here," Joan said, walking around her. "You aren't good for Brian. You won't accept the reality that he is mentally disturbed. And if he stays here in these mountains, he will never get any better."

Maybe I won't either, Jackie thought dismally as she watched Joan disappear around the side of the cabin. Maybe I'll just keep on loving Sam, grieving for Brian and be miserable till my dying day.

Shortly Joan came back carrying Brian, who, to Jackie's utter amazement, was kicking and thrashing as she held him, arms waving wildly. His mouth was wide open in a silent scream, and tears were running down his cheeks.

Joan was struggling to hang on to him. Her husband saw what was going on and leaped out of the car to come to her aid. As he carried Brian to the car, still fighting, she turned on Jackie to hiss between clenched teeth, "Do you see what you've done? He has never, ever acted like this. He has never fought me, fought anyone, but you've turned him into a holy terror with all your pampering and coddling.

"Maybe he does understand part of what people say to him," she rushed on, not giving Jackie a chance to speak, "and you have, no doubt, talked against me…against his father, and turned him against us. I hope you're happy."

She started for the car then whipped about to cry,

"And another thing. You're greedy. Just like Libby Pratt. You have no right to this land. It's Colton land and always will be. My son has told me you're planning to break off from the farm, and I've told him I'll give him the money to sue you for what's rightfully his."

Red-faced and shaking in her designer original from head to toe, Joan got in the car.

Seconds later Jackie watched, dumbfounded and rocked to the core, as they roared down the road and out of sight.

Sam had told his mother everything.

And her being so nice at first was all an act to get Brian out of there as quickly as possible.

But all of that, including the mean things she'd said, was not what had Jackie so tied up in knots. It was seeing how Brian had acted, how he had tried to scream…tried to tell his grandmother he did not want to go with her. That was not the behavior of a retarded child. It was the act of a child silently crying out for the help no one would give him.

And Jackie was powerless to do anything about it.

Madeline's letter was still on the table next to the rocker where she had left it. Sitting down, she picked it up and read it again.

They wanted her back.

And maybe that was where she belonged.

At least she would be far, far away from her dreams and far away from Sam and the joy they had shared for a little while.

She went inside, took up the phone and dialed Dove Haven's number from memory.

Maxine Dwyer answered and squealed to hear it was Jackie. "Oh, it's been so long. We missed you, girlfriend. What's up?"

She told her she wanted to speak to Madeline, and Maxine squealed again.

"Oh, I'll bet I know what this is about. She told us she was writing to you to see if you wanted your old job back. This is great, Jackie. Hang on. I'll put you through. It's going to be wonderful having you back. I can't wait to tell the residents. Only a couple have passed away since you were here, and—oh—I've got Madeline. 'Bye."

Madeline was just as pleased to hear from her as Maxine had been and told her that yes, she could have her old job back, except that she would have to report for work right away. "The dietician didn't work out her notice, leaving us in a bind. I hate to put pressure on you like this," Madeline said, "because I know you've probably got things to take care of up there before you leave, but the administrators are coming down on me hard over all this, and I've got to hire somebody fast."

"Don't worry," Jackie said without hesitation. "There's nothing to take care of here."

Sadly, it had all been taken care of.

There were no loose ends. Sam didn't give a damn and never had. Brian was leaving tomorrow.

And so was she.

"I'll be there," she said.

"Well, I know it's sudden," Madeline pointed out. "So if you change your mind, let me know so I can hire this other girl."

"Will do."

Jackie hung up and spun about, wondering what she should do first, then realized there really wasn't anything to do. Now that all the seedlings were gone, her only responsibility was a geranium in the kitchen window that she had bought for a little color on a blah winter day.

She was not about to take any of the furniture, which had already been there except for the mattress. About all she had bought was the faux fur rug, and she sure as heck didn't intend to take that. Every time she looked at it she thought of lying on it naked with Sam so many steamy nights.

Looking around, she decided there was absolutely nothing to take but her clothes.

Then she saw the little rolling pin on the windowsill. Despite having shared absolutely none of Libby's affinity for the place, she would take it with her as a memento of Libby.

But there was one thing she would need to do and that was run into town to the bank and close out her account. Even though there wasn't much money left in it, there wasn't a branch in Durham so it was best to take it all with her.

It was late when Jackie got to town. She had packed her clothes and then given the cabin a good cleaning. It was her intention to call Mr. Burkhalter and tell him he could let the animal shelter know they could take it over and do what they wanted with it. Let them fight with Sam and his mother.

She parked in front of the Book Nook, which was next door to the bank.

Willa saw her and ran to the door, calling, "Don't you dare go home without coming in to talk to me, Jackie. I haven't had a good chat with you in a long time."

The last thing she wanted was to get tied up with Willa, but knew she couldn't leave without saying goodbye.

As soon as she finished at the bank, she went into the

book store. And the first thing Willa said was, "Don't you go thinking harshly of Joan now. She told me about the little upset you two had this morning and regrets it. She's just so upset over little Brian that she gets carried away sometimes."

"It's all right, really." Jackie was glad no one else was around to hear such personal talk. "And I'm sure she's very nice otherwise."

"She is. Some of that money she married into might have gone to her head, but that's the way it affects some people."

Willa handed her a mug of coffee. Jackie took it and sank down next to the pot belly stove, which was still fired up. It might be spring by day but nights could be chilly.

"So how are things out your way?" Willa settled beside her. "Hank told me about the roof caving in on your hothouse and how you lost all your seedlings. That's a shame, but it was old. You can always rebuild."

"No, I'm not going to." She decided to get it over with, gulp down her coffee and be on her way. "As a matter of fact—"

Willa cut her off, "You know, I'm real put out with Sam. He's not treating my niece very nice. She took care of him back when he had the flu. Bonnie was also down with it and couldn't look after Brian, so Rosemary just moved in over there, and—"

The bell over the door jingled, and Willa glanced up, then cried, "There he is now." She stood to wave him over. "Get yourself over here. I want to tell you how rude you're being to Rosemary after all she did for you when you were sick."

Jackie's heart slammed into her chest. Sam, holding Brian's hand, walked over but did not sit down. He avoided looking at her as he said to Willa, "I haven't felt like calling anybody. I'll get around to it. Now did those books you ordered for Brian come in? He's leaving with his grandmother tomorrow, and I was hoping he could take them with him."

Only then did he glance Jackie's way, and she wondered whether it was her imagination or if he really looked ashamed.

"Well, I'll go see," Willa said, and got up to do so.

"I've got to be going," Jackie said to no one in particular as she stood.

Sam stepped in front of her. "Jackie, wait. I heard about what happened earlier with my mother, and I'm sorry. She's just so stressed out over Brian."

"It's all right," Jackie said coolly, cordially. "I understand. I had no business interfering."

She bent down to give Brian a big hug, blinking back tears as he hugged her back. "You be a good boy, you hear? And get well soon."

Sam patted Brian's shoulder, making his voice light and upbeat. "He's going to come home for Christmas next year in time for the parade, and I'll bet he'll be singing carols right along with everybody else, won't you, son?"

Jackie decided to get it over with. "Well, I won't be here to see it. I'm leaving."

Sam registered astonishment. "What...what are you talking about?"

She straightened, giving her hair a toss and forcing a smile to tell him, "You were right, Sam. I'm not staying. I don't like it here. I hate the weather...hate the isolation. I'm going back to Durham, to my old job, where I belong."

"But...but the farm," he sputtered. "What about—"

"You're going to have to work that out with the alternate beneficiaries. It's up to them. I'm out of it.

"Goodbye, Brian." She bent to give him a quick kiss and then hurried on her way before she burst into tears.

"Stay here, Son," Sam instructed Brian, and followed after her.

He caught up with her at her truck.

"Now what's this all about?" He put his hand on the door so she couldn't open it. "I thought you swore you'd never leave."

She shrugged, "I guess it's like you said. I'm a city girl." She flashed a sardonic smile. "I don't like not being able to have a pizza delivered."

She gave the door a yank, and he stepped back but said, "If this is because of the argument we had over those trees, we can work something out, Jackie. As for the ice storm, Hank told me about the roof caving in on your hothouse, and I was really sorry to hear it. I know you worked hard. I wish I could have helped, but I was sick and, oh, hell—" he gave a ragged sigh "—if you like the place, you should stay. After all, it's yours."

"Is it?" she cried. "I don't think so, Sam. That land will always belong to the Coltons, regardless of whose name is on the deed, and you and I both know it.

"But I don't care," she said, on a roll and unable to stop, "because I'm sick of frozen water heaters, roofs caving in, lights going off and having to carry wood in every day. I'm sick of broken fingernails, doing without because I forgot something at the grocery store and it's too damn far to go back and get it. So you can have your mountains, Sam," she finished, sliding into the truck and turning the key in the ignition to start it up, "because this flatlander is going home!"

She couldn't get away fast enough, hating herself for her lies. Nothing she said was true. She didn't mind any of the inconveniences she had endured, because she loved everything about the mountains...about her home.

Only it would not be her home much longer.

One more night, and it would all be over.

Sam watched till the taillights on the old truck disappeared. He felt no satisfaction in the realization he'd been right about believing Jackie would ultimately leave. Because somewhere along the way he had freed himself of the ghosts of the past and fallen in love with her.

Only now she was leaving, and there was nothing he could do to stop her.

And he supposed it was best he had taken sick and not gotten around to seeing her to tell her how he felt. She might have stayed on Brian's account, and that would never have worked.

No, it had to end, and now he was faced with trying to get over his broken heart.

Chapter Sixteen

Jackie put her suitcases on the back of the truck and tied them down so they wouldn't bounce off. Then she took one last walk through the cabin to make sure everything was secure and that she hadn't forgotten anything.

She also took a stroll around the yard, trying not to cry, because crying gave her a headache, and she needed all her wits about her for the drive to Durham.

So she wept on the inside, instead, because it was breaking her heart to leave.

Yet to stay would only bring deeper anguish. Being around the man she adored, unable to help the child she couldn't love more if he were her own, was more than she could bear. Kevin and all the woes he had inflicted was a piece of cake compared to this.

But then she had never loved Kevin the way she loved Sam.

And had not known what it was like to love a child.

The morning was glorious, the sun just beginning to peek over the eastern ridges, a lavender mist whispering through the grass.

The trees smelled extra sweet and fresh in the crisp air, and she drank deeply. She knew, beyond a doubt, that for the rest of her life every time she caught the scent of a Christmas tree, she would be reminded of this place that had been her home…her paradise…if only for a little while.

She knew she had to get on the road. She wanted to be in Durham by lunch, because there was much to do. And first on the agenda was finding an apartment, this afternoon, if possible, so she would be ready to go to work tomorrow.

With one last look around she opened the door to the truck, put one foot on the running board…then paused.

She had heard something, coming from the direction of the path between the rows of blue spruce.

She shook her head and climbed into the truck. Was it just the wind or her imagination, because who would be calling her·name at this hour? And why?

But then she heard it again and turned to stare in heart-jamming wonder when she saw it was Brian. And he was running as fast as his little legs could carry him, racing straight toward her.

"Don't go," he cried, tears streaming down his face, his arms outstretched. "Don't go…Mommy."

Jackie gasped and leaped from the truck to drop to her knees and gather him in his arms.

He burrowed his face in her neck, and she held him close for long precious moments, wondering if he had really spoken or if she had dreamed it amidst the shock of seeing him.

"I don't want..." he whispered brokenly, anguish mirrored on his cherubic face as he drew back to look at her, "I don't want to lose another mommy."

"Oh, my God." Jackie was all but crushing him she was squeezing him so hard. "Oh, my God, I don't believe it."

She managed to carry him up the steps to the front porch and sat down in a rocker. Over and over she crooned to him, telling him not to cry.

"I...I can't help it." He rubbed at his eyes with his little fists. "I...I stayed awake all night thinking about you leaving. And you can't, Mommy. You just can't."

He burst into fresh tears and threw himself against her.

Jackie was reeling. He could talk...and he had called her mommy...had begged her not to go...said he didn't want to lose another mommy. Oh, dear Lord, what was she to do? She could not abandon him now, and she had to stop Sam's grandmother from taking him away, because there was no need, and—

She heard the roar and looked up to see Sam's truck coming up the road, dust flying beneath the speeding wheels.

He braked to a stop and jumped out and ran to the porch, taking the steps two at a time. "I'm sorry, Jackie, but Brian climbed out his window, because he was locked in his room. It's a wonder he didn't break his neck going down the trellis. He knew my mother was getting ready to leave and was taking him with her, and he doesn't want to go, but—"

"He doesn't want me to go, either," she said quietly, looking him straight in the eye. "He said so."

Sam backed up a few steps. "He did what?"

"He spoke," Jackie said, continuing to hold Brian tightly. "He asked me not to leave."

Sam moved on shaking legs to sink down in the chair next to her. "I don't understand."

"I do," she said, smiling through her tears as she reached to squeeze Sam's hand, because he looked so pale and shaken. "He heard me tell you yesterday that I was leaving this morning. He thought about it all night and knew he didn't want it to happen. Something inside him was triggered to make him speak, or maybe he's been talking to himself all this time and nobody heard him. I'm afraid I'm clueless, because I'm not a psychiatrist—like your mother pointed out to me—but I think I know what's happened here. And I think Dr. Valcross will confirm it. Come inside. We're going to call him. I haven't had the phone disconnected, thank goodness."

Sam followed her but made no move to take Brian from her arms. It would have taken some doing, anyway, because he was hanging on for dear life and would have had to be pried loose.

It was early, and Dr. Valcross was not in his office. Jackie left word with his answering service, saying it was kind of an emergency, then coaxed Brian to let her go so she could find the makings for coffee. She and Sam needed something, maybe even a shot of brandy if she could remember where she packed the bottle.

Sam remained in a daze, walking about in circles and pausing now and then to stare at Brian and shake his head again. Finally, worriedly, he pointed out, "He isn't talking now. Are you sure he's okay? I mean, this is crazy."

"I'm sure."

Brian was sitting at the table watching them. Sam went over and took a seat next to him on the bench. Placing a hand on his shoulder, he softly asked, "Son, will you talk to me?"

Brian pursed his lips, then asked, "Will you make her stay?"

Sam's eyes filled with tears, and Jackie's heart went out to him. She went to his side and put her arm across his shoulders. "It's going to be all right, Sam. You won't have to send him away now. And I can come back and visit."

Brian's lower lip began to tremble. Jackie knew he wanted more than visits, but it was all she could offer.

As though he were a soul mate, able to feel and know her every thought, Sam caught her hand and squeezed it. "He wants more than visits, Jackie. And so do I," he added, voice cracking.

Jackie forgot to breathe as his words hurtled through her like a roller coaster running wild within her veins. What did he mean? She dared not ask, for fear she was reading too much into all of this, that he meant something altogether different from what she was thinking, hoping....

"Don't you realize I don't want you to leave, either...that somewhere along the line I fell in love with you?"

She took a deep breath and swayed.

He was on his feet in an instant to grip her shoulders and hold tight. "I know you only wanted the land...wanted me to teach you everything I knew about trees. But the life isn't for you, and you had to give up and go back to your world. So I can't ask you to stay, not even for Brian's sake, but you have to know that I do love you, Jackie, and I always will."

It was her turn to be speechless. Her head was spinning, and her heart was bouncing around in her chest like a Ping-Pong ball.

For the second time in a matter of minutes Jackie

thought she had to be dreaming. "Did…did you just say what I think you did?"

He nodded, devouring her with his eyes.

With a cry of joy she threw herself into his arms. "Oh, Sam, don't you know the only reason I was leaving was because I thought you didn't love me, and I couldn't bear to be around you, believing that? I love you, too. And I love it here. It's my home. I don't want to leave. I never did."

He gazed at her in wonder, and then their lips met, held, in a kiss of longing, a kiss of promise…and a kiss of hope.

Suddenly, they both felt it and sprang apart—tiny hands slapping at their legs as Brian begged to be a part of it all.

Laughing and crying all at once, they eagerly reached down to scoop him up and hold him between them.

Their bliss was interrupted by the phone.

Jackie ran to answer. It was Dr. Valcross, and she quickly told him what had happened.

He listened, then said, pleased, "Well, I'd say you've been dealing with psychogenic aphasia for sure. Sometimes it's called shock aphasia." He explained that in certain cases a terrible shock could cause a person to stop speaking, subconsciously fearing that if they did speak, it would somehow cause them to relive the trauma.

"Evidently," he continued, "Brian had begun to love you like the mother who abandoned him, and when he was faced with losing you, he had to relive it whether he wanted to or not. So he was forced to do the only thing he could—beg you to stay, which meant talking. I'd say you've nothing to worry about," he concluded.

"He should be fine. It's just one of those miracles that modern medicine can't explain."

When Jackie hung up the phone, she stepped eagerly into Sam's waiting arms. "It's going to work out, Sam. I just know it is," she said fervently.

Then, remembering his mother, she worriedly said, "But what about your mother? She might not be glad I'm staying. She doesn't think I have any more right to this land than Libby did. And I don't want hard feelings."

"We can change all that if you're agreeable."

"What do you mean?" She hoped he wasn't going to bring up the subject of a contract again.

But that was not at all what Sam had in mind.

He smiled, the dimple she adored appearing at the corner of his mouth. "Simple. We'll draw up one deed with both our names on it. Then no one can challenge ownership of these lands ever again.

"Because, my dearest," he cupped her face in his hands and kissed her again, "I want to give you a very special 'happy' if you'll have it—a wedding ring."

Epilogue

Sometimes spring cruelly bypasses the mountains. Winter yields to summer, with nothing in between but rain and warm temperatures that tease by day but plunge to freezing at night.

Nature, however, decided to be good to Jackie and Sam.

Spring came almost with a vengeance, the hillsides exploding with the brilliant pink blooms of the mountain laurel. Thick bushes that had sheltered wild animals through the cold months were alive with the gorgeous flowers of the rhododendrons.

Jackie had wanted to be married on the grassy knoll near the rushing stream beside the cabin. Sam agreed it was ideal.

Willa led a parade of well-wishers from town, and they turned the lawn into a rainbow of tents over food-laden tables for a feast after the ceremony.

Willa sighed as she helped Jackie adjust the train of her wedding gown. "This is the prettiest gown I've ever seen, and I think you're the prettiest bride."

They were in the bedroom of the cabin. Jackie thanked her and gave her a hug. She was proud of the gown she had chosen. Fashioned of ivory lace, it was studded with pearls. The sweetheart neckline was accented by the pouffed sleeves, which tapered to her fingertips. The skirt cascaded to a dramatic train, but it was lifted ever so slightly in front to show the tips of her ivory satin shoes.

Outside, a blue-grass band was tuning up, and Jackie laughed. "Not exactly the wedding march, but who cares? I'm a mountain girl now."

"That you are," Willa said, nodding her approval. "And we're all glad, too. But what's this about a honeymoon cruise?"

Jackie explained how it was Sam's way of saying that maybe they should get off the mountain once in a while, that he was willing to travel, do things, meet new people. She yielded because she knew it made him happy but knew she didn't care if she never left the Blue Ridge again as long as they were together.

"Hello? Can I come in?" Sam's mother knocked on the open door, took one look at Jackie and cried, "Oh, you are beautiful."

Jackie smiled, not certain what to do or say. She hadn't seen Joan since the day she'd come to the cabin to get Brian.

Joan crossed the room. She was holding a little white box. "Please wear these. They belonged to my mother."

With shaking fingers, Jackie opened it to see a lovely strand of pearls with matching eardrops. "Oh, Joan, thank you so much," she murmured through a mist of tears.

"Welcome to the family," Joan said, hugging her, then stepping back to wipe at her tears with a hanky. "I hope we'll be good friends, Jackie, and I'm sorry if we got off on the wrong foot."

"We will be," Jackie assured her, smiling all the way from her heart.

Together, hand in hand, they went outside.

It was time for the wedding to begin.

Jackie thrilled at the sight of Sam, so handsome in a dark suit, white shirt and tie.

His eyes glistened as she walked toward him, and she could feel his love wrapping around her like the majestic Blue Ridge Mountains that surrounded them.

When their vows were spoken, and it was time to exchange wedding rings, everyone gasped out loud with delight as Brian stepped forward. On a pink velvet pillow, he carried the gold bands.

Then, pronounced man and wife, Jackie and Sam sealed their pledge of love with a kiss...and promptly reached down to lift Brian up into their arms to be a part of it all.

"Your child," Jackie whispered, "is now our child, and I will love you both forever."

* * * * *

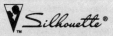

If you enjoyed what you just read,
then we've got an offer you can't resist!

Take 2 bestselling love stories FREE!

Plus get a FREE surprise gift!

Clip this page and mail it to Silhouette Reader Service™

IN U.S.A.	**IN CANADA**
3010 Walden Ave.	P.O. Box 609
P.O. Box 1867	Fort Erie, Ontario
Buffalo, N.Y. 14240-1867	L2A 5X3

YES! Please send me 2 free Silhouette Special Edition® novels and my free surprise gift. Then send me 6 brand-new novels every month, which I will receive months before they're available in stores. In the U.S.A., bill me at the bargain price of $3.57 plus 25¢ delivery per book and applicable sales tax, if any*. In Canada, bill me at the bargain price of $3.96 plus 25¢ delivery per book and applicable taxes**. That's the complete price and a savings of over 10% off the cover prices—what a great deal! I understand that accepting the 2 free books and gift places me under no obligation ever to buy any books. I can always return a shipment and cancel at any time. Even if I never buy another book from Silhouette, the 2 free books and gift are mine to keep forever. So why not take us up on our invitation. You'll be glad you did!

235 SEN CNFD
335 SEN CNFE

Name	(PLEASE PRINT)
Address	Apt.#
City	State/Prov.	Zip/Postal Code

* Terms and prices subject to change without notice. Sales tax applicable in N.Y.
** Canadian residents will be charged applicable provincial taxes and GST.
   All orders subject to approval. Offer limited to one per household.
   ® are registered trademarks of Harlequin Enterprises Limited.

SPED99   ©1998 Harlequin Enterprises Limited

Return to Whitehorn

Look for these bold new stories set in beloved Whitehorn, Montana!

CINDERELLA'S BIG SKY GROOM by Christine Rimmer
On sale October 1999 (Special Edition #1280)
A prim schoolteacher pretends an engagement
to the town's most confirmed bachelor!

A MONTANA MAVERICKS CHRISTMAS
On sale November 1999 (Special Edition #1286)
A two-in-one volume containing
two brand-new stories:

"Married in Whitehorn" by Susan Mallery
and
"Born in Whitehorn" by Karen Hughes

A FAMILY HOMECOMING by Laurie Paige
On sale December 1999 (Special Edition #1292)
A father returns home to guard his wife and child—
and finds his heart once more.

*Don't miss these books, only from
Silhouette Special Edition.*

Look for the next **MONTANA MAVERICKS** tale, by
Jackie Merritt, on sale in Special Edition May 2000.
And get ready for
MONTANA MAVERICKS: Wed in Whitehorn,
a new twelve-book series coming from Silhouette Books
on sale June 2000!

Available at your favorite retail outlet.

LINDSAY McKENNA
continues her heart-stopping series:

MORGAN'S MERCENARIES
III
THE HUNTERS

Coming in October 1999:
HUNTER'S PRIDE
Special Edition #1274

Devlin Hunter had a way with the ladies, but when it came to his job as a mercenary, the brooding bachelor worked alone. Then his latest assignment paired him up with Kulani Dawson, a feisty beauty whose tender vulnerabilities brought out his every protective instinct— and chipped away at his proud vow never to fall in love....

Coming in January 2000:
THE UNTAMED HUNTER
Silhouette Desire #1262

Rock-solid Shep Hunter was unconquerable—until his mission brought him face-to-face with Dr. Maggie Harper, the woman who'd walked away from him years ago. Now Shep struggled to keep strong-willed Maggie under his command without giving up the steel-clad grip on his heart....

Look for Inca's story when Lindsay McKenna continues the MORGAN'S MERCENARIES series with a brand-new, longer-length single title—coming in 2000!

Available at your favorite retail outlet.

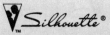

SDMM2

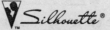

Of all the unforgettable families created by
#1 *New York Times* bestselling author

NORA ROBERTS

the Donovans are the most extraordinary. For, along with
their irresistible appeal, they've inherited some rather
remarkable gifts from their Celtic ancestors.

Coming in November 1999

THE DONOVAN LEGACY

3 full-length novels in one special volume:

CAPTIVATED: Hardheaded skeptic Nash Kirkland has *always*
kept his feelings in check, until he falls under the bewitching
spell of mysterious Morgana Donovan.

ENTRANCED: Desperate to find a missing child, detective
Mary Ellen Sutherland dubiously enlists beguiling
Sebastian Donovan's aid and discovers his uncommon abilities
include a talent for seduction.

CHARMED: Enigmatic healer Anastasia Donovan would do
anything to save the life of handsome Boone Sawyer's
daughter, even if it means revealing her secret to the man
who'd stolen her heart.

Also in November 1999 from Silhouette Intimate Moments

ENCHANTED

Lovely, guileless Rowan Murray is drawn to darkly enigmatic
Liam Donovan with a power she's never imagined possible. But
before Liam can give Rowan his love, he must first reveal to
her his incredible secret.

▼ *Silhouette* ®

Available at your favorite retail outlet.

COMING NEXT MONTH

#1279 THE NO-NONSENSE NANNY—Penny Richards
That Special Woman!
When pampered heiress Amber Campion took on the job of temporary nanny, she soon realized she was in way over her head. But somehow the kids' devoted uncle Cal always managed to soothe her frazzled nerves. She'd foolishly walked away from the sexy sheriff once, but *twice?* Not on her life!

#1280 CINDERELLA'S BIG SKY GROOM—Christine Rimmer
Montana Mavericks: Return to Whitehorn
Lynn Taylor's fantasy-filled date with Ross Garrison was a fairy tale come true—until the Whitehorn gossips got wind of their "affair." To save face, the virginal beauty reluctantly agreed to a pretend engagement to her dashing Prince Charming. But could they live happily-ever-after for *real?*

#1281 A ROYAL BABY ON THE WAY—Susan Mallery
Royally Wed
Against his better judgment, levelheaded rancher Mitch Colton agreed to help beguiling Princess Alexandra of Wynborough find her missing brother. But he never dreamed that their smoldering attraction would result in a royal baby-to-be....

#1282 YOURS FOR NINETY DAYS—Barbara McMahon
Ellie Winslow thought she'd seen it *all* since opening her halfway house for troubled teens. Everything changed when mysterious Nick Tanner became a part of her makeshift family. Her rational side cautioned that the hard-edged stranger was off-limits, but her heart wasn't listening....

#1283 PREGNANT & PRACTICALLY MARRIED—Andrea Edwards
The Bridal Circle
When rodeo cowboy Jed McCarron's heroics led the whole town to believe he was betrothed to pregnant doc Karin Spencer, he found himself playing the part of adoring fiancé—and doting daddy-to-be—a little *too* well.

#1284 COWBOY BOOTS AND GLASS SLIPPERS—Jodi O'Donnell
Although she was dubbed a modern-day Cinderella, suddenly single Lacey McCoy vowed to shed the regal typecast. Trouble was, no one back home believed her—especially Will Proffitt, who insisted the slipper still fit. So she set out to prove to the sexiest cowboy in the Lone Star State how wrong he was!